The

WRIGHT
LOVE

The WRIGHT LOVE

K.A. LINDE

Visit my website at www.kalinde.com
Cover Designer: Sarah Hansen, Okay Creations.,
www.okaycreations.com
Photography: Lauren Perry, Perrywinkle
Photography, www.perrywinklephotography.com
Editor and Interior Designer: Jovana Shirley,
Unforeseen Editing, www.unforeseenediting.com

ISBN-13: 978-1948427227

To all those who have lost and learned to find love again.

One

Sutton

My knees hit the ground in front of my husband's grave.

I clutched a bouquet of white flowers in my hands. Their blooms were bright and full of life, destined to shrivel and die long before their time. Just like my Maverick.

A tear slipped down my face even though I'd sworn I wouldn't cry. Not today. Not any more days.

A year of crying was enough for me. An endless year of tears brought on by memories, certain smells, the look on my son's young face, or sometimes from nothing. Just sitting in the car, waiting for the light to change. Not a thing running through my mind. And then the tears would hit.

How cruel could this world be that it would take my husband from me after only a year and a half of being married? Only a year with his son? Only twenty-four short years on this earth?

I placed the bouquet in front of his gravestone and traced my fingers over the engraved lettering.

Maverick Wright. A good husband and father. Gone too soon.

I couldn't recall if I'd chosen those words. The days and weeks after Maverick had died on the Fourth of July were a blur. My family in and out, Mav's family hovering, casserole dishes and church services and so much therapy. All I really remembered was holding Jason, crushed to my chest, as we'd buried his father and the love of my life six feet under the earth. Exactly where I was now.

A sob escaped my throat. My hand flew to cover the sound.

"A year," I whispered. "A whole year without you, Mav."

It seemed impossible.

Totally impossible to be here today and think that I'd made it that long.

When I'd first found out I was pregnant, everyone had assumed that I'd get rid of it. I had money. I hadn't needed to be shackled to my college boyfriend because of one little hiccup. But I never considered it. I loved Maverick with all my heart, and the baby had felt inevitable.

Sure, I had been scared as fuck. Terrified that we weren't ready. Worried about what other people would think. Upset by everyone's reactions. But I never doubted Maverick. Everyone had spouted bullshit about him knocking me up on purpose for my money, for that bold Wright name that came with so much respect in my hometown of Lubbock, Texas. I'd just known it wasn't true. Not only had Maverick been completely devoted to me, but I'd also utterly belonged to him. Our nerves had morphed into excitement, and when Jason was born, it was the best day of our lives.

Thirteen months later, Maverick was gone, and suddenly, I was a widow and a single mom.

My life couldn't have changed more.

"I survived," I told Maverick, sinking back on my heels. "That's about as much as I can say. I survived, and Jason survived. I never thought I could do it without you, but...but I did."

I felt guilty, saying it.

He was gone, and somehow, I was still functioning. Not the same. Not by a long shot. The Sutton Wright who had first married Maverick no more. Yet I was still making it day to day.

"I know you'd want me to be happy. But, God, I miss you every day. Being happy seems like such a stretch. Like, what is happy without you? I want to be able to get back to the good, Mav, but everything hurts. Sometimes, I wake up in the middle of the night to check on Jason, and I think I hear your voice downstairs. I rush down the hall, my heart in my throat, and all I find is an empty living room. And it hits me all over again that you're...you're never coming back."

I pressed my forehead into the grass that had grown over the empty pit where they'd put the casket. My tears stained the earth. I hoped that they reached him down there.

"No one understands," I told him, confessing my truth. "People don't get what I feel. All my friends are happy and young and living this beautiful life that we had, and they can't comprehend what I'm going through. That I'm a shattered mess inside. That just because I can manage a fake smile doesn't mean I'm okay. Christ, even when I manage a real smile, I'm not okay.

"Annie is still around, of course, and my family. And I made a new friend in the nanny, Jenny. I know we weren't close in high school, but I'm a different person now. All our friends from Tech," I said, my chest aching as I remembered the wonderful years we'd spent together at Texas Tech University, "they're gone. I was too much for them. Eventually, they got tired of my grief. It was easier to avoid me than anything else. They couldn't comfort me, but it was nice to have people nearby. And, sometimes...it's easier to have no one. To sit at home alone and feel numb. But I try not to, Mav. I know you'd want me to live. You always said I was so full of life. I don't know what you'd think of me now."

I rolled over and lay on back on the grave. I didn't care who stumbled across me lying there in my black sundress. The stifling hot July sun was streaming down onto my pale skin, which hadn't seen the sunlight in months. One look at me would probably be enough to convince someone to stay away.

"But I can't move on. That's what people say in so many words. God wouldn't give me more than I could handle. Everything happens for a reason. You'll find love again." I pressed my hands into my eyes. I'd been smart enough not to wear mascara to this. "None of those things are comforting. What kind of God would take you from me? What the hell kind of reason could there have been? And do I ever want to find love again?"

I lay there and spilled my heart to him. That was one of the best parts about Maverick; he had always been a great listener. I'd never shut up before, so that had been a great trait. I needed it now more than ever. Who knew that finding my own silence would only make me appreciate him more?

"I want to feel more than this again," I confessed.

Slowly, I sat up, keeping my back to his grave. I hated saying these words to him, but I needed to. I needed him to know. I needed him to understand. I wasn't abandoning him. This wouldn't change how I felt about him. But I needed this.

"You'll always be a part of me, Maverick. You'll always hold a piece of my heart. I could never replace you, and I don't want to. But I think...I think I need more. I'm only twenty-four years old. I can't stay in this place forever. *Moving on* is the wrong phrase. All moving on means to me is a plea to stop talking about it. My grief makes others uncomfortable, and they can't handle it. That's not my problem. It's theirs. What I want is..." I choked on finding the right words.

Silently, I slid back around to face him. I couldn't hide. Not from him. "What I want is to open a new place in my heart. To carry you with me and find a way to keep living. Because, right now, I'm barely making it."

I wiped a tear from my eye and waited for divine intervention. Something to tell me I was making the right choice. I could already hear all the people judging me for moving on with my life after being a widow for only a year. That wasn't long enough. Not by a long shot.

But they'd be wrong.

I was still in mourning for Maverick.

I could mourn him and grieve for him and find a way to do more than just survive this cruel fucking world.

I wanted to find a tiny piece of the butterfly inside myself that had once been so joyous. The wings were broken. It couldn't fly anymore. But, somewhere deep down inside, it needed to heal so that I could spread my wings once more.

"I love you." I placed a kiss on his tombstone. "I'll always love you."

Then, I gingerly got to my feet.

My fingers clenched the heated stone. I wished more than anything that I could hear his voice one more time. Just once.

I didn't even remember the last thing that he'd said to me a year ago. I'd gotten to the Fourth of July parade early to secure a spot. I'd kissed him good luck, and he'd disappeared for the marathon with my best friend, Annie. A few hours later, he was gone. Heart failure. Undetected heart condition. Nothing could be done.

As if that was a comfort.

"I know what we had was beyond compare. I'll never have that again. But…maybe I can have something else." I closed my eyes against the onslaught of emotions. "I'm sorry, Mav. I'm so sorry."

With a heavy heart, I glanced once more at his gravestone, hoping to see some sign that he understood. But nothing came. He was silent.

If I wanted to find a way to live, I'd have to do it myself.

Just as I'd done everything during the last year.

Without my husband.

Two

David

A year. A whole year since I'd interviewed to be the CFO of Wright Construction and gotten the hell out of San Francisco. It had been a snap decision, but it was a fucking miracle that I was out of Silicon Valley.

No one had understood why I was so dire to leave. I'd made a name for myself there. With the trajectory I had been on, I could have taken over the town in a few more years. Then, I'd left it all behind. Everyone had thought that I was insane for taking the Wright job.

Maybe they were right.

Not that I cared.

I'd needed a fresh start.

Middle-of-nowhere West Texas seemed as good of a place as any.

I glanced around the desolate terrain from the driver's seat of my Ferrari. The Wright brothers' trucks and SUVs dwarfed my shiny red sports car. I couldn't have felt or looked any more out of place.

A hand slapped down on the roof of my car, startling me out of my thoughts.

"Coming inside or just moping out here all day?" Morgan asked as I rolled down the window.

Morgan Wright was the CEO of Wright Construction and my boss. She was also probably the closest thing to a real friend I'd had in years.

"Probably the latter."

"Fitting," she scoffed.

"Where did you come from anyway? I don't even see your car." I clicked the door open and stretched my long legs out of the seat. The tiny Ferrari was not conducive for my height, but I couldn't give it up.

"I've been here most of the day. But Patrick just showed up." She beamed.

"Ah. He's not tired of you yet?"

Morgan rolled her dark eyes. "Whatever, Calloway. You're just jealous."

I shrugged. It wasn't a lie. Morgan and Patrick had started dating six months ago. For everyone who knew them, it had been a dozen years in the making. That kind of relationship was always to be envied.

Morgan opened her mouth, likely to rag on me again, but my phone started ringing in my pocket. I slipped it out of my gray dress slacks and glanced down at the number. My lips pursed.

"Come into Jensen's when you're done, okay?" Morgan said, gesturing to her eldest brother's mansion.

I nodded, and then she hurried out of the summer heat. With a sigh, I silenced the ringer on my phone and waited for Katherine's call to go to voice mail. *Why the hell is my sister calling?*

I hadn't heard from her in over a year. We weren't what you would consider close. She was the perfect daughter, and I was…far from the perfect son. It wasn't a good day when our paths had to cross. Not because I didn't care for her, but she was always the bearer of bad news. And I didn't know what she could want from me after such a long stretch of silence.

Nothing good. Nothing I'd want to deal with.

I'd left for a reason, and I'd be just as happy to stay out of it. She already knew that though. No use in beating a dead horse.

A few seconds after the call ended, a notification blinked for a voice mail. I breathed out heavily through my nose and pressed the phone to my ear.

"I know you're avoiding my call, David. I'm not going to talk about this in a voice mail. Just call me back." There was a slight pause. "I miss you."

With a shake of my head, I stuffed the phone back in my pocket. Clickbait voice mail. Well, I was definitely not going to call now. Not when I was about to walk into a Wright party. Especially not on the Fourth of July. Not when today was the day that Sutton was suffering.

And I knew she was.

She had to be.

No one could go through what she had gone through and not be upset on the anniversary of her husband's death.

By some strange twist of fate, I'd been there on the day it happened. I could only come in for my interview on the weekend of the Fourth of July.

9

Jensen and Morgan had brought me along to the parade. Maverick had collapsed while running a marathon and died that morning.

And, now, I was coveting his wife.

Fuck.

Just…fuck.

I turned back to the house, determined to ignore the conflicted feelings I had for Sutton. That wasn't what she needed right now.

Three quick horn blasts jolted me before I made it to the door. I swung back around and found Sutton's blue Audi TT pulling into the driveway. She parked next to my Ferrari, and I admired the sight. The woman had good taste in cars.

She stepped out of the driver's side and waved. "Hey, David."

"Sutton," I said with a head nod in greeting.

Sutton fussed over Jason while his nanny, Jenny, jumped out of the passenger seat with a dessert tray in her hand. Once Jason was on his feet, he ducked out from under Sutton's arms and raced straight toward me.

"Yes!" he cried dramatically.

I laughed and scooped him up into my arms. Jason was my buddy. Before Sutton had gotten a full-time nanny, I'd babysat for her a couple of times. I knew it was important for her to get out.

Jenny huffed and passed the dessert to Sutton. "I'll get him."

"No, Jen!" Jason said, vehemently shaking his head as she approached.

"Come on, Jason. Let's go get some lunch. You're hungry, right?"

The kid was always hungry. That was a given.

10

I gently passed him over to Jenny, and they disappeared inside, leaving me alone with Sutton. That was when I got my first look at her. She was standing in a beam of sunlight. Her brown-to-blonde hair was expertly curled around her shoulders. A thin layer of makeup only enhanced her natural beauty. Her pink lipstick drew my eyes. The black sundress she was wearing was nothing special, yet…she took my breath away.

She was starlight on a cloudless night.

And I directed my sails by her beacon.

"I can carry that for you." I stepped forward and took the dessert tray out of her hands.

She smiled softly. "Thanks."

I saw then all the pain she was holding in. Once upon a time, I'd seen a genuine smile from Sutton. A year ago, she'd looked up at me from a blanket on a marathon track, and her radiance had shown through. Her head haloed by light, she had been so full of joy and on top of the world.

Now, her cheeks were hollowed out. She'd lost weight. She was a shell of the butterfly I'd seen that day. Yet still beautiful and surviving and alive. She was getting through one day at a time, and I couldn't ask for more than that.

Though I wanted to.

A part of me yearned to be the person to put all the pieces back together. To never see her in this much pain again. To get her to smile like that one more time.

But not today.

"You ready?" I asked instead of voicing my swirling thoughts.

She took a deep breath and then let it out. "No."

"We don't have to go in."

Her blue eyes looked up into mine. A tumultuous sea in the midst of a hurricane. "We do. My family wants to be there for me."

"Your grief belongs to you. You choose who you share it with."

"It can't be shared, only survived."

"Sutton…" I began.

"Ah! There you are!" a voice cried from the doorway.

We both turned to find Sutton's best friend, Annie Donoghue, emerging from the house. She was a tall redhead with a vibrant personality. She had also been running the marathon with Maverick a year ago. She and Sutton had only gotten closer throughout the year. Tragedy brought people together like that.

"Hey, Annie," Sutton said with another sad smile.

"Are y'all going to come in or what?" Annie asked with her Southern lilt.

"Definitely," Sutton said. "We were just catching up."

"Awesome. Hey, David."

"Annie," I said.

My eyes met Sutton's one more time. Something passed between us. A shared moment acknowledging that she was doing this more for her family than for herself. I understood it. They wanted to help her. She didn't want to be alone at home, crying all day. Even though it would have been acceptable.

Instead, she put on a brave face and entered the house.

I followed behind her, carrying her dessert tray in my hands and wishing I could explain how much I understood. And how much I wanted to help.

Three

Sutton

"You look really great," Annie gushed. She plucked at the black dress I'd put on this morning to go to the cemetery.

"Thanks."

"Is this new?"

I shook my head. I'd gone through a phase of buying a whole new wardrobe to replace everything I'd ever owned when Maverick was alive, but that had been this winter. I had gotten past that by the time I needed sundresses and sandals.

"Well, I want to borrow it. I wish my ass wouldn't hang out of the back."

"Curse of the giant."

"Luck of the pixie," Annie joked back.

Annie had been a lifesaver during the last year. Always quick with a smile and a promise of a night out. Eager enough with a girls' night in with Jason when life had started weighing on me too much to go out. She was the best friend a girl could ask for.

"I'm lucky to have you."

"Psh!" Annie said. "I love you, girlie. How was this morning?"

I shrugged my shoulders. What was there to say? Talking to Maverick had been…necessary, cathartic, wonderful, horrible, painful. It had been everything I needed in that moment and nothing. God, what I wouldn't give to hear his voice one more time. One of his goofy laughs. See a teasing smile.

But, no, I would never have any of that again.

I'd known it for a long time, but there was a difference between knowing and *knowing*. Today…I *knew*.

"I've had better days," I finally answered.

"Yeah," Annie agreed. "You'll get back to better days. I know you will."

I swallowed back a comment. I was tired of hearing that I was going to get better. Even from Annie, who was one of *the* most supportive people in my life.

Was I doing better? Yes.

Was I going to suddenly wake up one day and *be* better? No.

Shit didn't happen like that.

Sometimes, I wished more people were like David. He was so calm and understanding. He never said the things that other people said. He just let me feel how I felt. No bullshit. No expectations. It was a relief.

We meandered into Jensen's kitchen where Jenny was fixing a plate for Jason. He was munching on some strawberries and eyeing the cake in the corner.

Jensen's fiancée, Emery, had a sister, Kimber, who owned a bakery downtown. She must have brought one of her signature Death by Chocolate cakes for the party. David followed behind me and placed my brownie tray next to her cake. It looked so elementary in comparison. At least they tasted really good. That was all that mattered.

"Cookie," Jason said.

"Later," I said, passing Jason another strawberry off the platter. "Jenny is making you a plate first."

Jenny finished Jason's plate and then took his hand. "Come on, little dude. Let's go see your aunt and uncles. I think Kimber brought Lilyanne and Bethany, too."

I grabbed a bottle of water and followed behind them. Kimber's youngest, Bethany, was only six months older than Jason, and they played together all the time. As soon as he was outside, he ran straight toward her, ignoring both his food and the rest of the family who wanted to see him.

"Is it too soon to begin talks of an arranged marriage?" Kimber asked, appearing at my side.

"Never too soon. Look at how cute they are together."

"She's probably going to run all over him. I mean…she's a handful."

"Jason is like a perfect kid," I told her. "I guess I got lucky."

"Lilyanne was like that. It's a trick. They make you think all children will be like that, so you have another one. And then the second is a hellion."

"Sounds right. The universe is like that."

"Speaking of…how are you today?" she asked with a smile.

15

"Been better honestly. Jason helps. Baking helps. Getting out of the house helps."

"Baking?" Kimber quirked an eyebrow. "I know a thing or two about that."

I threw her a half-smile. "Yeah. I've been baking a lot to keep busy when I'm at home. It's therapeutic."

"That it is. Well, if you want to come work at the bakery with me, there's always a spot for you."

"What? Really?" I asked in disbelief.

"Of course. No strings attached. If you hate it, you're off the hook. But I can always use another hand. Especially with the college students starting back up in a month," she said, referring to Texas Tech University, which was across the street from her adorable bakeshop.

A year ago, I would have laughed at the thought of working in a bakery.

Six months ago, I wouldn't have been able to pick myself up off the ground to make it to a job.

Yesterday, I wouldn't have thought that I'd even want to work.

I was the only Wright in my family who had never held down a job. I'd been flighty as a kid, jumping from one activity to the next with equal parts enthusiasm. I'd dropped out of college to have Jason. But I always had the trust fund to fall back on when I refused to work for my family's company. It always felt too cliché to jump into the family job. I wasn't Morgan by any stretch. I wasn't like any of my siblings in that regard.

But, now...

I'd told Maverick this morning that I wanted to live.

Maybe working with Kimber at the bakery would be just the opportunity I needed to start fresh.

"Actually…that sounds great," I told Kimber. "Like really, really great."

"Seriously?" Kimber asked.

"Yeah. When do I start?"

"How's next week?"

"Excellent."

"What's so excellent?" Jensen asked.

He appeared then before us with the rest of my family in tow. Jensen owned his own architecture company after relinquishing control of Wright Construction to Morgan. He'd proposed to Emery at the grand opening, and their wedding was coming up.

"Sutton is going to come work for me," Kimber said.

"Wait, what?" Morgan gasped. She flicked her long brown hair out of her face in disbelief. "You'll work for Kimber but not me?"

"And this surprises who?" Austin asked. My sarcastic and broody older brother had recently gone through a stint in rehab for his alcoholism but was doing tremendously better.

But it was the youngest brother, Landon, who responded, "No one. Literally no one."

"Just because you're back professionally golfing again doesn't mean that you can be a shit," Morgan said.

"Uh, I think that's precisely what it means."

Couldn't get all of us together without an argument breaking out. Old habits died hard.

"Children," Jensen said with a sigh and then a laugh.

"Sutton started it!" Morgan teased.

"Actually…" I began, knowing she was playing because I was the easiest target. I always had been.

I was the baby.

In every sense of the word.

Jensen had all but raised me. Our mom had died when I was just a year old. Our father had been a raving alcoholic and succumbed to the bottle before my twelfth birthday. Vices ran deep in our family.

Unfortunately, I knew exactly what it was like for my son to grow up without a parent. The only difference was that he didn't have siblings to help him along. I had four. They were wild and prone to addictions with skeletons in their closets, but they were mine. And I loved them.

"Leave Sutton alone," Jensen said with a smile.

"I can't help that she decided to take a job with Kimber behind my back," Morgan groaned. "What's the fun of being CEO of a company if I can't hire my little sister?"

"I'm pretty sure you worked your whole life for this, and like a crazy person, you think it's all fun," I said.

"Well…yeah. If we're going to get into specifics."

"Ignore her," Austin said. He nudged Morgan out of the way. "There are more important questions to consider."

"Like?" I asked, already knowing I would regret asking.

"What are you baking for me?"

"I brought brownies."

"Did someone say pot brownies?" Landon asked.

Austin's eyes rounded in mock surprise. "Landon Wright! How dare you say such things in front of the children." He pointed at me. "Virgin ears."

"Don't you have to qualify for your next golf tournament anyway?" Jensen dryly asked Landon.

"Details," Landon said with a lopsided grin.

"But, wait…are they pot brownies?" Austin asked.

"No!" I groaned. "And I'm not making them at Kimber's. Don't scare her away from me already!"

"Yeah, it's her first job. Give her a break," Jensen scolded them.

"Oh God," Emery said, coming up to his side. "Are you wagging your finger at people? Do I need to extract you from the situation?"

"Probably," Morgan said.

I shook my head at my large and outrageous family. It was moments like these that reminded me why I'd shown up at all. Sometimes, it was easy to forget that other people had been affected by Maverick's death. That sounded selfish, even to my ears, but it was more like self-preservation. My pain had been so all-consuming. It still baffled me sometimes that people could draw me out of it again.

My family especially was good at it. We'd always been close. Everyone had a place in the family, but I was just stumbling into my new role. Finding a place to be now that I wasn't the vivacious, bubbly sorority girl. But they all still loved me, no matter where I fit.

"Your sis offered Sutton a job," Morgan said like a proud parent.

"At the bakery?" Emery asked. "That's awesome! I'll get to see you more."

I grinned. "That'll be good. Right up to the wedding."

"Kimber is making the cake!"

"All in black?" Morgan guessed.

Emery shrugged, her smile going as wide and mischievous as a Cheshire cat. "Maybe. Don't tell this one." She pointed back at Jensen.

"As if he would deny you anything," Morgan said.

"He wouldn't," I confirmed in a small voice. My throat closed around the words. I'd made it through the word *wedding* without choking up. But talking about it...I still wasn't okay. "Excuse me. I'm just going to..." I threw my thumb behind me and made a hasty retreat.

I was glad that I had only dusted on some waterproof mascara when I went home to pick up Jason. I pressed the palms of my hands into my eyes as I closed and locked the bathroom door. My breathing was uneven. I tried sucking in a few quick breaths to keep tears from falling again. I'd wanted to be strong here. That was what I needed.

With a frustrated slam of my fist on the granite countertop, I cursed this feeling.

My eyes were red and puffy. I hardly recognized the face looking back at me. When had I deteriorated this far? I wished that my brain could get with the picture. I was ready to be a human again.

Yet...I wasn't. Not yet.

It took me a while to get myself back under control.

Only when I felt certain I could go out and enjoy the party did I leave the bathroom. When I walked out, I was surprised to find David standing there.

"Oh, sorry." I stepped out of the way.

"No, I was waiting for you."

"Did you...need something?"

"Just wanted to see how you were doing. I saw you made kind of a speedy exit."

"Emery was talking about the wedding," I confessed to him. Normally, I wouldn't say anything, but it was so easy to talk to him. "Just…hard sometimes. You know?"

"I do."

"I'm not an asshole for resenting all my siblings' happily ever afters?"

"You probably wouldn't be human if you didn't. I know I envy what Morgan and Patrick have. They're so happy all. The. Time," he said with round eyes. "I mean, Morgan is probably my closest friend, but I can only stomach so much of it."

I laughed a brittle thing. "Yeah. And here we are. The odd ones out."

His stare penetrated deep into me at my last words. I didn't know what had compelled me to say it. It wasn't as if David were a pariah. He was a good-looking guy. He was a CFO of a Fortune 500 company. He had everything going for him. He should be happy with someone who deserved him.

So, why was he standing here in front of me?

My heart stuttered. A blush crept into my cheeks. I sucked my bottom lip into my mouth and suddenly felt as if my limbs didn't quite fit my body.

There David was. My friend. A constant companion through the last year. He towered over even Jensen, easily dwarfing my small frame. His hair was dark blond and gelled to perfection. His eyes were a hazel brown that changed with his mood. Right now, they were nearly gold from the afternoon sun shining in from the windows. And his fashion was even better than my own. Gray slacks and a blue button-up, the sleeves rolled up on his muscular arms.

He was…David. Just David.

Yet…that look.

I instinctively took a step back as embarrassment washed over me. "Well…thanks for checking on me."

Awkwardness crashed down between us for the first time since I'd met him. A tension that had never been there before. That suddenly enveloped the short distance that separated us. It vibrated and rippled as if it had its own substance. As if I could reach out and touch it. Feel it solid beneath my hand.

He didn't say anything. His eyes stayed firmly fixed on mine. I knew that I should say something else. Take another step back. Walk away from that look. No one had looked at me like that in a year. With something other than pity. With something other than sadness.

This was…wrong.

It was wrong, right?

There should be no tension.

When I'd told Maverick this morning that I deserved to live my life again, I hadn't thought…this. I'd had nothing concrete in mind. Was this his answer? Or was I just a total asshole for still standing here?

Finally, David took his own step back. "Anytime, Sutton. You know I'm here if you need me."

"Right," I said, loosing a quick breath. "Right. Of course."

Then, I hurried past him like a crazy person and back outside.

I was ready to live again. I wasn't ready for…that. Whatever *that* was.

Four

Sutton

It wasn't long before everyone was complaining of the oppressive summer heat. The kids were the only ones who didn't want to come inside, but Jason was already pink from the sun. Kimber and I put Jason and Bethany down for a nap, which we were sure they were going to wake up from at any minute. It took longer than normal to calm him down, and I went back downstairs, exhausted. I plopped into a chair in the dining room and pretended not to listen to Jensen's conversation.

"No. No, we'll get on the phone tomorrow. Morgan and I will come by to hear the details." He sighed heavily in frustration. "I can't believe we weren't informed about this. Yeah, I know that. Yes, I know I'm still on the paperwork filed at court. Fine. Yes. Have a good Fourth. Thanks for letting me know."

"Everything okay?" I asked after he hung up the phone.

He gritted his teeth. "Van Pelts."

"Oh God," I groaned. "New development?"

"Come on. Apparently, it's on the news."

I followed him into the living room where he flipped the channel to the news.

"Hey! We were watching that," Austin complained.

"Just wait for this," Jensen ground out.

And everyone quickly shut up at Jensen's tone. It wasn't often he got upset. It had to be something serious for that to happen. Like his ex-wife, Vanessa, or someone messing with Wright Construction—like the Van Pelts.

They were a family-run New York City–based investment firm. A staple of the Upper East Side, a conglomerate of wealth, which had risen to even higher heights amid the '90s economic boom.

My father had invested millions with them under the guise of new development. In reality, the Van Pelts had been sucking up money from every avenue possible and working a Ponzi scheme. My family's money had disappeared long before we knew what they'd done. Long before it came out almost a decade ago what the Van Pelts had been doing. Long before their CEO, Broderick Van Pelt, was imprisoned for fraud and stripped of pretty much everything he could touch, leaving his family penniless.

We never got our money back from the Van Pelts. Though Jensen had sued the hell out of them. We were just lucky it hadn't wrecked the company— like so many other companies. In fact, Wright had only grown from there, but it should have been the

24

sign that my father wasn't fit to be CEO. By the time Jensen had found out what exactly our father had done, he was six feet under the ground. Just another thing he'd never have to atone for.

A breaking news update flashed on the TV.

"Parole hearing set to take place next week for the man convicted of millions of dollars of investment fraud. Broderick Van Pelt was arrested and later sentenced to fifty years behind bars. On Friday, Van Pelt called in, trying to convince parole board members he'd been locked up long enough after spending eight years in prison. We're awaiting news from the New York State Division of Parole for further updates on the status of Van Pelt."

The room had gone utterly silent. Even those who weren't aware that the Wrights were a victim of the Van Pelts' scheme could tell that something significant was happening.

The television showed a video of Broderick from the day he had been sentenced. I'd seen it before. Along with the image of him in a suit and tie as a successful investment banker that the media always used in place of his prison mug shot. Because…of course.

"Bastard," Morgan snarled, jumping to her feet.

"Trying to sweet-talk his way out of prison," Austin grumbled. "What an asshole."

Landon sighed and pinched the bridge of his nose.

"I'm already in contact with our lawyers. They called me and asked me to take point on this because I filed the lawsuit. But I can hand it over to you, Mor?"

"No, let's do it together," she said.

He nodded. "We'll have to go in next week. It never ends."

"I'd be happy to."

"Um…what am I missing?" Julia asked from the couch next to Austin.

"They took millions from us in the early 2000s," Austin filled her in.

"Yeah, really screwed us over," Morgan said. "Just what we need to deal with after Owen was here last year."

She was still bitter about our uncle after he tried to take the company away from her. I didn't blame her.

"Well…what a day, huh?" I muttered with a sigh.

Everyone's attention veered over to me. And then I saw it…on everyone's faces—pity. Ugh, my least favorite thing to see. I'd grown really, really used to seeing it, too. I could spot it a mile away. My family wasn't even trying to mask it. They looked at me as if I were linen threatening to blow away in a light breeze.

"Sorry. You shouldn't have to deal with this today," Jensen said. "I should have thought—"

"No. It's fine. I mean…none of us should have to deal with any of this at all, but it's not like Dad gave us a choice."

"True, but—"

"It's okay," I said quietly. I avoided everyone's looks and raised my chin, determined not to run away. "It's a new year. I'm going to be okay."

Austin and Landon shared a look of disbelief. Morgan shared her own with Patrick. Everyone clearly disagreed with me.

"Whoa," Annie said, appearing then as my savior. "What did I miss?"

"Nothing," I said.

"Sutton," Jensen said with worry in his eyes. He'd played the role of parent so long that it fit him like a glove.

"I'm okay, Jensen. I'm okay."

He sighed and nodded.

Annie gripped my elbow and pulled me out of the living room. I rested my head on her shoulder.

"I wish everyone wouldn't treat me like I was an invalid."

"You kind of are an invalid," Annie said playfully. "Jenny, tell Sutton that she's an invalid."

"I think you're doing better today than you have in a long time," Jenny said. "You seem lighter since this morning."

I heaved a sigh. "It was good to talk to him. Even if he doesn't answer. But I think it's time to finally start living again. I'm not...past it or anything. I just don't want to be an invalid forever."

Annie brushed my hair off my shoulder. "You're doing great, sister. Promise. You'll know when you're ready."

A fear crept up in my chest at the next thought. "What if people think it's too soon?"

"No one can judge you for how you feel," Jenny said kindly.

"It's just...Maverick's parents."

"They cannot blame you for having a life, Sutton," Jenny said, tucking her blonde high-low bob behind her ear.

"Well...they *can*."

"They shouldn't," Annie said.

"I'm supposed to have dinner with them soon. They wanted to see me this weekend, but I knew I wouldn't be up to it."

"I've got an idea. How about you don't worry about everyone else? The only person you can control in this situation is yourself," Jenny said.

Annie nodded. "It's not like you're replacing Mav or forgetting him. You're young and beautiful, and you can't stay locked up in your house forever."

"You're right," I said with more conviction than I'd felt when I brought it up. "I kind of love y'all."

"We know," Annie said with a grin.

Jenny rolled her eyes. "Oh, Annie."

"This is why you hated me in high school."

"I didn't *hate* you."

"Y'all," I said, stepping between them.

"Right. Not today," Annie said. "Tomorrow, I shall discuss all the ways that Jenny was a total weirdo in high school."

"And I shall discuss all the ways Annie was the class slut."

I tipped my head up to the ceiling and blew out a breath. My two best friends. Lord, help me.

They might rankle each other, but they both loved me and would be here for me through anything. That much they'd proven over the last year.

A few hours later, Jason was fast asleep, curled up on a blanket at my side. A cool breeze skated in during the evening. Lubbock might be a dry and dusty climate, but it boasted some of the best sunsets.

Orange and pink and yellow blanketed the sky as we all waited for the fireworks display to begin.

My fingers circled through Jason's hair, which was curling at the edges. He was growing up so fast. It was as if I'd blinked the last year away, and suddenly, he was already so big. It was unfair that I had to watch time slip away. I wanted to hold on to him just like this forever. Every mother's wish, I guessed.

The kaleidoscope of colors hung heavy in the sky when I felt the blanket shift, and David sat next to me. He'd excused himself earlier this afternoon and been on the phone for a long time. I'd kept my distance from him after that weird instance in the house. I didn't know what it meant or if it was really nothing at all. I wasn't the best judge right now, and considering everything else going on…

Well, my head could have made the whole thing up.

He stretched his long legs out ahead of him, and his hazel eyes glowed a perfect strain of gold in the setting sun. His hair blew gently with the wind.

"Hey," he said with that kind smile he always reserved for me. Not pitying, just pleasant.

All awkwardness from earlier evaporated. It was just me and David again.

"Hey."

"Little guy's all passed out."

"Yeah. He barely napped. And, usually, he's out at least an hour in the afternoon."

"Too much excitement."

I nodded. "Mostly Bethany."

"Poor kid. He's in for a rude awakening when they grow up."

"Pretty much," I said with a laugh, glancing down at my sleeping toddler.

"Hey, Sut?"

My eyes crawled back up to his. "Yeah?"

"I want to apologize about earlier."

"Oh?" My cheeks heated.

"I know today is hard on you, and I wanted to make sure that you were all right. I think I hovered and made you uncomfortable. I would never want to do that to you. Especially today of all days. I felt horrible and tried to give you the space you needed."

"Oh," I said again dumbly.

I *had* misjudged that look from David. There was no moment at all. He was worried about me, like he always was, and wanted to make sure that I was all right. It had been nothing. Definitely nothing worth thinking about.

I didn't even know what had given me that awareness of him. I knew, of course, that Morgan had mentioned that there might be something between David and me. Now, it was clear that whatever Morgan had thought was also false.

He saw the broken china doll and wanted to help pick up the pieces. For a friend.

And I appreciated that about him. His strength and the care he took in everything he did. I'd just thought there was something else there for a second. But I was wrong. I used to be better at that kind of thing. Apparently, I was way out of practice on reading people.

"I can leave you be if you want me to," David offered slowly.

"No," I said at once. "No. I like having you around. You didn't make me uncomfortable at all."

Tension fell away from him all at once. His shoulders relaxed. A breath released from his lungs. A smile crooked the corner of his lips. His eyes were inviting.

"Good. I'm glad."

He touched my shoulder in a friendly gesture. A weird flutter sparked in my stomach. Like the first beat of an unused drum as it cleared the dust away.

Then, his hand disappeared, and he turned back to face the now inky-black sky. Stars twinkled in the pitch-black night. It took me another second to turn away. To not overanalyze what had just happened. To accept that this was okay. That I had misjudged David, and he had no interest in me other than as a friend. And I had no interest in him…either.

As the first firework burst in the sky, I wondered how much of that was a lie.

Five

David

I'd fucked something up.

Made a misstep somewhere on the road that I couldn't figure out how to come back from. I'd thought that I was walking a straight line, but it turned out I was on a hiking trail with no beginning or end. Just an endless, winding middle.

In the last year, I'd grown to call Sutton my friend. I'd be lying if I said I was okay with losing that in the hopes of having more with her. But the fear in her eyes on the Fourth of July two weeks ago had been enough for me to pull the emergency brake on my Ferrari and come to a screeching halt.

Metaphorically speaking.

But the truth was, two weeks had gone by, and I still missed her. She had started working at Kimber's bakery, Death by Chocolate, and even though she'd said that what had transpired between us didn't make her uncomfortable, I'd carefully avoided the place to give her the space I thought she wanted.

Up to a point. Up until now.

Maybe I was a jackass for reaching out to her again after the awkwardness of the Fourth, but I had done it anyway. Now, after hours of working with Morgan on a new contract, I was finally leaving work and picking Sutton up for lunch with me. I'd been sure to invite Jason to put a barrier between us. I wanted to make things right, to get back on the straight and narrow with her. I didn't like being in this interminable middle. I hoped today would fix that.

The bell tinkled overhead as I entered the cozy and bright bakery. The place was packed, considering most of the students were out of town. All but one French macaron–inspired table was covered with textbooks and laptops. I stepped across the black-and-white-checkerboard-tiled floor and up to the glass display that revealed all the incredible sweets. But it was the woman standing behind it that drew my eye.

Short and sweet with her hair pulled up into a ponytail and a touch of blush on her cheeks. A mint-green apron wrapped around her trim waist. She smiled when she saw me.

"David!" Sutton said. "You're late!"

"I know. I'm sorry. Morgan."

She waved a hand. "You don't have to explain. I know my sister."

"How do you like this place so far?" I asked, leaning forward on the white granite counter.

"Oh, I love it!" she squeaked. "I didn't know I could enjoy something like this. I'd always thought I'd inevitably end up another brainless Wright sibling at corporate. This is actually…fulfilling. Kimber is training me in the back in the mornings, and then once customers are here, I take care of the front. I can't wait to bake full-time!"

"I bet that will be sooner rather than later."

"Keep your fingers crossed. Now, let me tell Kimber that I'm heading out for lunch." She disappeared into the back and returned a minute later, minus an apron, with her crossbody purse draped over her chest. "Ready?"

"Should we wait for Jason?"

"Oh! Right," she said, as if she'd just remembered. "Jenny had him down for a nap. She told me to go, and she'd get him lunch. So, it's just the two of us." She hopped out from behind the counter. "Where are we going?"

"Are you sure you still want to go?" I asked carefully.

I hadn't planned on us being alone. I'd thought having Jason around would prove that I wasn't trying to move in on her or anything. I'd also thought he might serve as a nice barrier between us.

But alone…well, that was something different. And I wanted to make sure she was okay with that.

"Oh my God, yes," she said, grabbing my arm and dragging me toward the entrance. "I'm starving. I need food, or I'm going to get stabby. You do not want to see me hangry."

"All right, all right," I said with a laugh.

"Are we taking your car?" she asked with eager eyes.

"We can take yours if you'd prefer."

"Are you kidding?"

"The Ferrari it is."

"You going to let me drive?" she teased.

"One day," I said as we approached my baby. "Maybe not in traffic though."

"I can handle a stick shift!" she cried.

It took every ounce of self-control in my body not to arch an eyebrow in her direction at that comment. To joke that I bet she *could* handle a stick shift.

She nudged my shoulder. "Oh, come on, laugh at me. That sounded bad, even to me."

My eyes met hers, and she was smiling broadly. A real smile. A full smile. Nothing fake or wary or fearful in that gaze. Not normal or back to whatever her normal had been, but I could see the new job had done her wonders.

"A stick shift?" I asked.

She shrugged. "It sounded better in my head."

"Just get in the car."

She laughed and plopped down into the passenger seat. I zoomed away from the bakery, glad that Sutton was in a good mood. Not that she was always depressed and crying or anything, but laughing hadn't been easy for her. And, now, we were going to lunch together as if everything were totally normal. As if we'd done that a hundred times before. As if there were never a barrier between us.

I parked outside of Torchy's, and we took a seat at the bar to order our tacos instead of waiting in line. Our guacamole appeared, and Sutton dug in like she hadn't eaten in days.

"This is amazing," she groaned. "I'm so glad we came here."

"It's nice that you have Jenny full-time to watch Jason."

"Oh God, I know. She's a lifesaver. Sometimes, I still can't believe that we didn't like each other in high school."

"Really?"

"Well, no. It makes sense. I was this bubbly cheerleader, and she was in the marching band and a theater geek. Our circles didn't exactly blend."

"Did you cheer with Annie?"

She nodded. "Annie was captain. I was never serious enough about anything to do that. I kind of floated along. Another reason Jen and I didn't click. She was one of those overachiever types who hated that I got whatever I wanted because of who I was."

"Well..."

"Yeah, yeah, I know. I was the worst," Sutton said, breaking off another chip. "I acted like that because my parents were gone, and Jensen was in college. I didn't know I was such an asshole."

"All high school kids are assholes. I promise you're not unique in that regard."

She snorted. "I bet you were a saint."

"About that..."

"Ohhh?" She raised her brows. "Do tell."

"I kind of ran in a bad crowd in high school. Most of my friends were drinking and doing drugs and hooking up with multiple women every weekend. We broke into a hotel once and got caught vandalizing the place, drunk and high and swimming naked in the pool."

"Oh my God!" Sutton gasped, cracking up. "You?"

I nodded. "We would have all been taken to jail if it hadn't been for one guy's parents being a local politician."

"Wow."

"Yeah. We all got off with a slap on the hand. The politician's son was the worst of the lot. Still is, to be honest."

"Oh, the life of the young, privileged, and stupid."

"Pretty much."

"And this was all back in San Francisco? That's where your family is, right?"

I stared down at my hands. "Yeah. My family is in San Francisco. Not that we're on speaking terms."

Sutton frowned. "I couldn't imagine not being on speaking terms with my family."

"Well, we had a falling-out. Pretty substantial one. It's one of the reasons I was quick to leave San Francisco and take this job."

"How does your sister feel about your move?"

My eyes darted up to hers. I'd never mentioned that I had a sister.

"Sorry. I might have accidentally eavesdropped when you were on that phone call forever on the Fourth."

"No, it's okay. We're not really speaking either. I hadn't heard from her in a year."

"Why?"

God, how to explain Katherine?

"She sides with our parents."

"I see."

"And I guess…she's getting married."

"Really?" Sutton asked, some of that wariness returning. "Is that why she called? When is that happening?"

"They don't have a date yet."

"You sound like you wouldn't go even if they did."

I made a face. "Undecided."

"She's your sister!"

"She's…well, Katherine is Katherine. If I showed back up, she'd find a way to try to make me stay. And I kind of like it here."

A smile played on my lips when I looked at her again. I liked being here. I liked being with Sutton. There was no way in the world I would want to go back to dealing with my family…even Katherine, who I did miss.

Her eyes were lowered with dark lashes playing across her cheeks. When she opened her eyes again, it was clear that she had interpreted my words the way they were intended. I should have been subtler. I should have held back. I shouldn't have been so direct.

But it had just slipped out. And she wasn't backing away. She wasn't closing in on herself. She was meeting my gaze.

It was as if something had shifted in the last two weeks. Something had shaken loose in her chest. Maybe it was the new job or being past the one-year mark or something…but she seemed as if she was more open.

Yet I still didn't push it. I didn't say anything further. I'd misinterpreted her gaze on the Fourth of July. I wouldn't do it again.

"Well," Sutton said, clearing her throat, "I don't want you to leave either, but you probably shouldn't miss your sister's wedding."

"Maybe I'll take you with me when the time comes, and you can meet her." I couldn't believe the words left my mouth, even as I said them.

"I'd like to meet her. That'd be nice."

Our food finally showed up, saving me from saying something else stupid. We dug into our tacos and let the conversation shift into mundane things like my job and how much she loved the new bakery and the new words that Jason had said this week. It seemed he was learning new words every day. He had a mind like a steel trap.

I paid for both of us against her objections. "You can get it next time."

"There's a movie I want to see. If you don't mind a superhero movie, I could get the tickets," she suggested with a nonchalance that could not be mirrored.

I stumbled on my step outside and caught the glass door. I played it off like a legitimate trip instead of shock at her words. Was she...asking me out?

"You do like superhero movies, right?" she asked quickly.

"I do in fact."

"Great. Friday?"

I chanced a glance at her, and she seemed completely with it. She wasn't growing a second head or anything. This was normal. She wanted to hang out with me. By her expression, it was clear that this would not be a date. Friends...again.

"Friday sounds great."

Six

Sutton

"Jenny, have you seen my brown Tory Burch sandals?" I asked, scanning the living room.

"You left them behind the side table."

"Of course I did." I circled the couch and found the mysterious sandals exactly where Jenny had said they were. I slipped my feet into them.

"Mommy!" Jason cried as he toddled into the living room.

"Hey, bud." I scooped him up in my arms and nuzzled his cute little neck. "Are you ready for your party with Jen?"

He nodded eagerly. "You pwetty."

"Aw, thanks, little dude." I glanced up at Jenny as I set him back on his feet. "I actually managed makeup today."

"You look great, Sut," Jenny said warmly. "It's good to see you looking a bit more like yourself. I hope you have fun on your date."

I froze in place, the smile slipping from my face. "Date?" I sputtered.

"Uh...yeah?"

Jason tugged on her sleeve, and she sank to her feet to play with his toy trucks. I saw the whole thing through a haze. Normally, I'd jump right in with them and have a ball. But, right now, I was...unraveling.

"It's not..." I shook my head. "It isn't...is it?"

"Well, I mean, I thought it was," Jenny said with a grimace. "If it's not, then it's not."

"We didn't say—I mean, shit!"

"Shit!" Jason repeated loudly.

I slapped a hand over my mouth, and Jenny stifled a laugh.

"We don't say those kinds of words. Only grown-ups do," she explained.

"Mommy did."

"Yes. Mommy is a grown-up."

He shot her what served as an exasperated look and went back to his trucks.

"Sorry," I muttered. "I don't think it's a date. Do you think it's a date?"

"Well, you got a sitter to go to the movies on a Friday night with a guy," Jenny said, leaving the statement hanging.

"Right...right," I repeated. "Of course. He probably thinks it's a date. Oh my God, I don't know how to date, Jenny. I don't want to date. I'm not ready."

"Calm down. Just breathe. It doesn't have to be a date."

"But it is. It's a date. I'm going to have to cancel."

"What?" Jenny asked in disbelief.

I sank into the couch and put my head in my hands. I didn't know why this hadn't occurred to me before. Of course it looked like a date from the outside. When I'd asked David to go to the movies, we'd just had such an incredible lunch, and everything had felt so normal. I'd thought I was going for an extension of what we were already doing that afternoon.

Not a…date.

A real-life fucking date.

I hadn't been on one of those before Maverick in…years.

"I can't do this."

"Sutton…you shouldn't cancel."

No, I absolutely had to cancel. This wasn't fair to David at all. I was a mess. A total hot mess. Maverick had only been gone a year, and no guy should have to deal with me in the middle of this.

I had just started my first job. That was enough new for one month at least. Working at Kimber's was amazing and refreshing in a way that I'd never known work could be. But that was entirely different than going on a date.

David was…no, I didn't even know what he was. Attractive, of course. Kind, sweet, happy, and kind of wonderful. That didn't mean I should date him. Or anyone for that matter.

No one would want all my baggage. I didn't even want all my baggage. And how could I really start over with Maverick still haunting me every night? With his son staring up at me from the floor of the house we'd bought together? With all the memories swallowing me whole?

I swiped my hands under my eyes and stood. My stomach clenched as I glanced around the house. A job was enough. Dating was…dating was something else.

"I'm going to go call him," I whispered as I disappeared into the foyer.

I heard Jenny sigh, but she could hardly blame me for being reticent.

David answered on the first ring. "Hey, Sutton. I'm not late again, am I?"

"No." I coughed to cover choking on my answer.

"Everything all right?"

"I…I have to cancel," I whispered hollowly.

"Oh," he said, his voice dipping in distress. "What happened? Are you okay? Was Jenny not free? We could stay in and hang out with Jason, if you'd prefer."

I closed my eyes over his kind words. Nothing had happened. No, I was definitely not okay. Of course, it would seem like it was something else other than my own brain turning traitor against me.

"I just…can't…do this."

"This?"

"Us."

He let the word hover through the phone. "I wasn't aware there was an us, Sutton."

"I don't know how to do this." My hand rested on my heart, and I leaned my head back as I tried to get words to form.

"There's a you, and there's a me. It can just be you and me."

"I'm not ready to date. I didn't realize that this was a date when I asked you. And, now, I realize it's a date. I'm a scattered mess, David. I feel like shit, and…God, now, I'm rambling." I took a deep, rattling breath. "I'm not in a good place. It would be unfair to you to have expectations that this is something other than friendship."

"Sutton, I didn't think that this was a date," he said calmly.

"You didn't?" I asked in horror.

"No. But, if you're worried that it is, we don't have to go. Or I can assure you that we're just going as friends. Or we can, again, stay in and hang out with Jason. There are no expectations here."

"Well…I just made myself look stupid."

My cheeks heated. I couldn't believe I'd freaked out on David on the phone before we were supposed to go to the movies. All because of the word *date*. And then he hadn't even *thought* it was a date. It was just something that Jenny had assumed, and I'd gotten it stuck in my head.

My panic attack had been for nothing.

"You don't look stupid. I understand why you would freak out about dating. You decide what you want to do, and I'll go with that."

I paced into the living room, and Jenny turned a not-subtle-at-all look of eagerness in my direction.

"Well?" she whispered.

I shrugged and waved her away, returning my attention to David, "I…I don't know. Do you still want to go?"

Jenny hissed behind me, "Go!"

I made a face at her, sticking my tongue out. Jason laughed from where he was seated and did the same. He was such a mirror at this age.

"I would love to go still, but if you're not comfortable, then we don't have to. It's up to you."

My heart pattered in my chest. He'd said it wasn't a date and that it could just be us going out as friends. Plus, I did want to see the movie. That hadn't been a lie when I asked him in the first place. It seemed a waste not to go when I had Jenny for the night. Maybe I was making excuses to still go.

But, with the scary word out of the way…it could be fine.

"Okay. Let's…let's still go," I told him.

"You sure?"

"Yeah. I was looking forward to it before I had a panic attack."

"All right. I'll be there soon to get you."

I hung up the phone and sank back down in the couch.

"I completely freaked out on him. Why does he put up with me?"

"Do you want the truth?" Jenny asked.

My heart skipped at the implication. Then, I shook my head. "Lie to me."

Jenny arched her eyebrow. "He's a really good friend, and he sees you as a little sister that he wants to take care of. It's nothing special. Your heart need not get involved."

If that was the lie, I definitely wasn't ready to hear the truth.

Seven

David

I knew this was a mistake.

The second I'd heard Sutton's voice on the phone, I had known that she was going to cancel. That the thought of us alone in a darkened movie theater was going to undo her. Even though we'd never made it seem like it was a date, the implication was there. And, when she'd realized, she'd done a complete one-eighty.

I was honestly surprised that she'd even decided to go through with it. It hadn't sounded like she wanted to. And, like the sucker I was, I didn't back out. I probably should have. It would have been easier for both of us.

Then, I wouldn't be sitting outside of her house in my parked Ferrari, trying to decide how to make this non-date not feel like a date.

Still, I stepped out of the car, made my way up the path to the front door, and knocked. I waited with my hands in my pockets. No flowers in sight. No expectations. That was what I'd promised. I could do this. The last thing I wanted was for Sutton to have a breakdown. She'd been through enough. I wasn't going to add more to her plate.

The click of the lock made me straighten my spine. Sutton peered out the door as if she didn't know it would be me standing there. Her bright eyes were round and rimmed with coal, her lashes long. Her lips were coated in a neutral pink color that did nothing but draw my attention to them.

"You made it," she said by way of a welcome. She dragged the door open wider.

"I did."

I got my first glimpse at the gauzy cerulean dress that matched her eyes and the way it made her pale skin almost glow in the low lighting. With her hair down and light makeup, she looked like a goddess straight out of Greek mythology. I gawked. I couldn't help it.

Thank God she wasn't looking at me.

"Jenny, we're about to leave. Do you need anything from me?" Sutton asked.

"Nope. I'm good." She turned to me. "Hey, David."

"Appreciate you helping your friend tonight, Jen."

"Anytime." She ruffled Jason's hair. "Say good-bye to your mom."

"Bye, Mom," he said, flapping his hands. Then, he ran and wrapped his arms around her legs.

She kissed the top of his head. "Love you. Pay attention to Jenny, and I'll see you later. Can you say bye to David?"

Jason smiled up at me. The kid was too cute. All chubby cheeks and fine, dark hair and all-seeing big eyes. He waved at me, too.

"Night, Jason."

Jenny pulled him back as Sutton exited the house. They waved us all the way back to my car. I popped open the passenger door for Sutton, who fidgeted with her purse and then sank into the seat. I realized as I closed the door behind her that I'd gone on autopilot and opened her door for her. Just as I would on a date.

I silently chastised myself and vowed to get it together before I jumped into the driver's side and veered toward the theater.

"The theater on University, right?" I asked just to verify.

Her head popped up. "Oh…no. I, uh, I got tickets to Alamo. I can't…go into the other movie theater anymore. Too many memories."

Oh. Maverick. She must have gone to the other theater with him. That made sense. It was the one where most of the college students went since it had the deep reclining seats and better specials.

"Sounds good. Alamo it is. I've been meaning to try it anyway."

She blew out a breath and then nodded. I could see her struggling to come to terms with actually being out with me. I was shocked that we had made it to this point myself. A year of pining after someone utterly unattainable had forced me to realize that this might never happen. It likely never would. No chance. Horrible for me to even consider the possibility.

Sutton Wright was a widow.

I didn't deserve this spark of hope for us. But I wasn't going to turn away now.

Our drive to the movie theater was filled with Top 40 radio and idle chitchat. She seemed nervous, and I didn't want to give her a reason to feel that way. I just wanted to enjoy my time with her. Date or no date.

Alamo Drafthouse wasn't like other movie theaters. There was no one waiting to check your tickets or a long line for concessions. Instead, there were Star Wars cardboard cutouts and a fully stocked bar. It was smaller than the other theaters in town, but the theater and its clientele liked it that way.

We made our way to our theater and found our seats in the top row. The patterned chairs were red to match the carpet and the walls with a raised table between every pair of seats. A waiter dutifully appeared at our table with a smile once we sat down.

He checked the tickets Sutton had purchased on her phone and then took our order. "If you want anything else, just stick an order card up."

Sutton nodded. "This place is the best."

"I already like it."

"Just wait until you try my root beer float." She groaned. "To die for."

"Noted."

I leaned back and waited for our food to get there as the theater filled to capacity. It was opening weekend for the latest Marvel movie. I was surprised she could get good enough tickets. I'd heard this place filled up. I said as much to her.

She blushed. "Uh…"

"What?" I asked, finding the slight blush on her cheeks irresistible.

"Okay, confession: I might…or might not have purchased these tickets two months ago when they went on sale."

"Two months ago?" My eyes widened in disbelief.

"Yeah. How the hell would I have gotten these seats at this time otherwise? Are you crazy?"

"Were you supposed to go with someone else?"

"Well…no. I mean…I bought two tickets together because I didn't want to go alone. But I didn't ask anyone else. Annie was always my backup."

"Uh-huh. Annie is the backup? You mean…Annie ditched you, and you invited me?"

"No!" she spat. "That is not what I mean. I'm glad you're with me. Annie just drools over the hot guys."

"And you don't?"

"Of course I do. But I also like the comics and the storytelling and the politics and the romance. I like all of it."

"Are we really here to stare at a Hemsworth brother?"

She fluttered her eyelashes at me. "Would you blame me?"

"I mean…he is pretty hot," I conceded.

She scoffed. "They're all stupid pretty. It's really not fair to have this many six-packs in one movie."

"Six-packs are so overrated."

"Totally," she said, waving her hand at me. "I mean, God, just look at you. Who wants that much muscle anyway?"

I couldn't help it; I burst into laughter. "You don't know I have a six-pack."

"Don't you go to the gym every morning?"

"Yeah."

I wasn't exactly a gym rat. But I was the kind of person who did my best thinking when my mind was otherwise occupied. I'd been running since I was a kid, and I never really stopped. The weights and toning had come later. I solved so many problems while on the elliptical or doing pull-ups or weighted crunches. It was part of my routine now.

"I've been around my brothers long enough to know the type of guys who go to the gym every day," she said with a smile. Then, she pinched my bicep.

Her touch sent a thrill through my whole body. Our eyes locked as the lights lowered to begin the previews. I knew I should look away. That would be the smart thing. Give her the space she needed. But staring into her blue eyes, I wanted nothing more than to lean into her, to make this more than it was.

I wouldn't. But I wanted to.

With a breath, I turned back to face the screen. The previews went by in a zip, and the movie began. I'd missed the last couple of movies before this one. But, even if I'd been following it closely, I'd have found it difficult to concentrate with Sutton sitting so close.

When we had sat down, the armrest between our seats was up. I didn't adjust it, and I waited to see if she would. But it stayed up the entire time. I didn't know if it was a clue, but fuck, it was hard, sitting here with her like this in a darkened room.

I could feel her presence so acutely next to me. As if we were both reactors with electricity tethered between us. Every time she shifted her body and leaned closer, I felt the zap.

Maybe it was elementary to be this intensely aware of her in a movie theater. To be fair, I'd never gone to the movies on a date before. It wasn't really something we did where I grew up. So…this was my first non-date movie moment. And I suddenly understood why kids all over the world were sneaking into movie theaters to make out. There was something genuinely tense, charged, and thrilling about this.

I inched a bit closer. She inched a bit closer. Our knees almost touched. I could feel the heat from her arm. My stomach knotted as I forced myself not to move. I wouldn't make the first move. That could shatter everything like a hammer to a mirror, followed by seven years of bad luck.

Sutton turned her head to look at me. I shifted my eyes to meet her gaze. Her mouth was open slightly, as if she had a question that she couldn't quite answer. She drew her bottom lip in between her teeth, and I couldn't help it; I glanced down at her lips.

I swallowed hard at the slight widening in her gaze. Then, I quickly looked away. If I kept watching her…if she kept observing me like that…I was going to kiss her. No doubt.

Then, I felt an even smaller shift, and then her pinkie was touching mine in the space between our bodies. She looped her pinkie over mine, and a shuddering exhale left her body. Something exploded in my chest at that one touch. That one move changed the entire dynamic of us forever.

I'd been wrong when I said I hadn't been aware there was an us.

There was definitely an us.

Eight

Sutton

"That was so excellent," I gushed as we exited the movie theater.

My heart was in a puddle on the floor next to me. It felt so exposed at the moment that it practically had its own zip code. I couldn't look directly at David. I couldn't do much more than bounce from foot to foot with excitement as we meandered back to his car.

"Better than the last one I saw."

I puffed out a breath. "I don't even want to know the last one you saw. They're all spectacular."

"I didn't know you were that into comics."

"I read them when I was a kid. I love the movies now. I'm a big X-Men girl. I always wanted to be Phoenix."

He clicked the Ferrari open and shot me an exasperated look. "Phoenix?"

"Oh, come on," I groaned. "Jean Grey? Telepath *and* telekinetic?" I rolled my eyes and waved him away when it was clear there was no recognition. "Hopeless. What did you do as a kid?"

He shrugged. "My parents were kind of strict. They wanted Katherine and me to grow up into version 2.0 of them, which basically meant that, when we were still in diapers, we had expectations about what Ivy we were going to attend. Not much room for comics and such."

"That sucks," I said, slinking into the passenger seat. "Did you end up going to an Ivy?"

"Yale."

I whistled. "Fancy."

He grinned as his eyes met mine, and I remembered then why I wasn't looking at him. Those eyes. Hazel. Sometimes green, sometimes blue, sometimes gold. They were molten right now, eyeing me like he wanted to devour me alive.

I quickly faced forward.

Something had changed in that movie theater. With the lights off and no room left between us, I'd let my guard down. I'd just enjoyed our time together. Sat through the movie and felt his presence, solid and whole next to me. Then, I'd done the unthinkable...

I'd reached out for his hand.

What had I been thinking?

No. The truth was...I hadn't been thinking.

For once in a year, everything had completely slipped away. All thoughts and feelings and guilt and fear had vanished. I'd been there, watching my most anticipated movie of the year, with a great guy, and it hadn't mattered then that I'd told him it wasn't a date.

The stars had aligned.

And it had felt right to bridge that distance.

My stomach had fluttered. My heart had leaped in my chest. My mouth had gone dry. But my hands had been steady, and I'd wanted it to happen. We hadn't moved the rest of the movie. Somehow, reality hadn't crashed back in until the final credits had rolled, the sneak peek of the next movie had finished, and we'd had to disentangle ourselves. Then, I'd gotten self-conscious again. I was already missing those couple of hours of surety.

I cleared my thoughts and went back to the matter at hand. "Did you major in business?"

"Of course," he said with a sigh. "My parents wouldn't have paid for anything else."

"Seriously?" I gasped.

"Yep. The only practical degree for taking over…" He paused. "They wanted me to work with them."

"Why aren't you?"

His hands clenched the steering wheel. "Wanted to make a name for myself on my own."

"I know what that's like."

"I suppose you do." He relaxed at that and then zipped out of the parking lot and back toward my house. "Why haven't you ever wanted to work for Wright?"

"Oh no, not you, too."

"I'm not recruiting you. I promise."

"It's expected of me. It's almost like I don't even have a choice in the matter. It doesn't matter that Landon went off and became a professional golfer; I'm still supposed to fall into line."

"That feels very familiar."

"Yeah, well, I don't know what anyone thinks about me working at the bakery, but it's better than Wright. Nothing wrong with the company. I love it. But it's not for me, and I never want to be forced to do something I don't want to do. Plus, I guess I am a bit contrarian."

"You?" he asked with a laugh.

"I have this habit of purposely doing the opposite of what people expect of me. The easiest way to make me do something is to tell me not to do it."

He arched an eyebrow. "Noted. We are *not* going to see the next superhero movie that comes out."

My eyes flashed in his direction. "What if I said I already had tickets for it?"

"No can do, Sut," he said with a mischievous grin. "Not your kind of thing."

"That's it. We're going." I crossed my arms over my chest. "You have no choice in the matter."

He chuckled. "Twist my arm already."

"You're going to regret this challenge."

His eyes said he highly doubted it. And I didn't mind that he'd effectively forced us into seeing him again.

Nerves hit me anew when we finally pulled up to my house. He parked his car out front, and before I could say anything, he dashed around the car to open my door. My breath stuttered as I allowed him to help me get out of the tiny sports car. He closed the door, and then there we were. Just casually standing together on the sidewalk. He gingerly reached forward and took my hand in his.

My eyes rounded, excitement and fear rippling through me. Our fingers laced together, and I reflexively took a step closer to him. His hand dwarfed mine, completely enveloping it. I liked the feel of my hand in his. His fingers were long, and his palm was hardened with calluses. It was warm and inviting against my soft, delicate hand, bitten-down fingernails and all.

I couldn't believe this was happening. I couldn't breathe. This was...too perfect.

He slowly walked me forward to my front steps. Our hands clasped the entire time. I wasn't ready to let go yet. This was a huge step, and I wanted to savor it.

"David," I whispered softly.

He brushed a stray piece of my hair out of my face. Lubbock wind was relentless, even in the rainy season. His hand lingered on my cheek, and I finally found the courage to look up at him.

His eyes were bright gold in the porch light. They spoke of devotion and desire. His face was so near mine. His body so warm. It had been so long since I felt anything like this.

A dull buzz rang in my ears as everything else slipped away. I wanted to reach out, and I wanted to stay put. I didn't know what to do. I didn't know what to say. All I could do was stare up at him, wavering with what my body was telling me.

"I really want to kiss you," he admitted.

I drew in a sharp breath. Those words shattered any illusion we'd put on this night.

"But this is all up to you." His hand moved to my jaw, slipped down my neck and over my shoulder, and reached down to grasp my other hand. "This is whatever you want it to be. Ball is in your court."

My body remained frozen as my heart melted at his words. I knew that I'd said this wasn't a date. But it'd been so obvious from the start that it was. Merely proclaiming that it wasn't hadn't done anything.

But being with David was effortless. I didn't have to think or agonize or freak out over anything. He just was, and we just were. That was enough.

I realized with a start that I didn't feel bad about us going out tonight.

Maybe I should have had a lingering doubt, but in that moment, alone with him on my front porch, I had none.

"Yes," I whispered. It was the only word I could manage, and it was enough.

David's hand moved back to my cheek. He drew me in a step closer to him. Our bodies nearly touching, our lips so near, our breath mingling tantalizingly close. My hand twitched into his shirt as anticipation coursed through me.

Then, his mouth covered mine. Soft, tender, and not an ounce of tentativeness. His lips were perfect, and they fit to mine like a jigsaw puzzle. I closed my eyes and fireworks exploded in my vision, molten joy poured into my heart, and heat spread through my core. This wasn't just a simple kiss. It was a totally new adventure. The start of something inconceivable and utterly unique. This was a new first kiss.

A new first.

As David pulled back, I ached for more. All I wanted to do was push back against him and demand more. Demand so much more. I had barely gotten a taste. I wanted this. It didn't feel fair that it could end this soon.

"Good night, Sutton," he whispered, pressing one more kiss to my lips.

"Good night," I breathed.

Then, he smiled a golden smile that nearly undid me and walked away.

I watched him until he was back inside his car. Then, I turned the handle on my door and walked inside.

Jenny was seated on the couch, watching Netflix and eating a bag of popcorn. Her own movie night.

"Hey!" she said, brightening. "How did it go?"

I plopped down next to her. That was when everything that had happened crashed down on me. Holding hands and kissing and dating. Having feelings for David and wanting another date and *wanting* another man.

Oh fuck! Oh fuck, fuck!

Without warning, I burst into tears.

"Oh, Sutton! That bad?" Jenny asked. She pulled me into her arms and put her chin on the top of my head.

I shook my head, tears uncontrollably running down my cheeks. "That good. That very, very good."

Nine

Sutton

"Why don't you go open up the shop? I can finish up here," Kimber said. With her back still to me, she pulled a selection of cupcakes out of the oven.

I carefully washed my hands and tried to smudge off a stray bit of flour from my cheek before making my way up to the front.

The weekend had been…quiet. After my breakdown with Jenny, I'd recovered and felt a smidgen better. Guilt still crept through me when I thought about what I'd done with David, but it had been nice. It had felt nice.

I shook my head as thoughts of David ran through my mind on repeat. We'd spoken a few times through text, but it was clear that he was giving me space to breathe. I appreciated it. Wrestling with my thoughts alone was hard enough.

Baking helped though. I had weekends off at Kimber's, but I'd come in bright and early Monday morning to get started. When I started baking, everything would shut off. It was blissful.

My mind was so far gone already that I didn't even notice that someone was standing outside the glass window until I flipped the Open sign over and unlocked the front door. Annie's smiling face appeared as the bell dinged overhead, announcing her presence.

"Hey, Annie. Coming to get some treats for the office?"

Annie had been working as a receptionist for a dentist for the last year while applying to medical school. I was going to miss having her around all the time when she started at Texas Tech this fall.

"Yeah. Do you have any of those little cinnamon-sugar doughnuts? And coffee. Dear God, coffee." Annie walked with me to the counter and propped her elbows on it to stare up at me. "I cannot wait to fucking quit."

"Another month?" I asked as I poured her a coffee and passed it over before getting to work on the doughnuts.

"The longest month of my life."

"Still going to be hooking up with your boss after this?"

She snorted. "Not bloody likely." She blew on her coffee and then downed it like a life force. "I'll probably get tired of him when he isn't an authority figure over me."

"You have such a problem with authority."

"Duh. Daddy problems."

I laughed. Because, by daddy problems, she meant she liked to date men old enough to be her father. Or really anyone she wasn't supposed to date.

Annie set the coffee on the counter. "Okay. I've waited long enough. A little birdie told me you had a date. I waited all weekend, and no call, Sut."

I blushed. Right. Of course Jenny had told her about it.

"It wasn't a date."

"Uh-huh."

"Okay…it might have been a sort of date."

"Spill."

"Nothing. We went to the movies."

"And…" Annie said, reaching across the counter to snag a doughnut.

"There was some hand-holding and one chaste kiss."

Annie squealed. "A kiss! I'm so happy for you, Sutton."

A smile grew on my face at her excitement. My stomach had been in such knots all weekend. Especially since Maverick's parents had called.

"Wait…why do you suddenly look sad?"

"Maverick's parents want to see me. I saw them after the anniversary, but I've kind of put them off since. I needed some separation."

"Let's not think about them right now. Let's think about the fact that you went on a date and it went well and you're happy about it. Is it going to happen again?"

"I don't know," I murmured.

"Well…do you want it to?"

I glanced down at the baked goods in my hands. My stomach fluttered at the thought of going on another date with David. With all the problems in my life, it was nice to think of having something that wasn't tied to that. Maybe it was selfish to want that for myself. But I couldn't deny that I did.

"Yes."

Annie grinned wide. "Then, do it. I'm sure he's nervous. If you want this, go for it. It'll be good for you to at least try again."

"You're right," I agreed. "That's what I told Maverick anyway. I want to try again. No one can fault me for that."

"They really can't."

I pushed the box of doughnuts over to her. "Mission accomplished, Donoghue. Now, get out of here, and go see that hot dentist of yours."

"He just loves my sweet tooth," she said with a wink as she hoisted the box in the air.

I laughed and shook my head at her. She was my best friend and nuts, but I loved her. I was glad to have someone to talk this out with because the ball was in my court. And I was ready to make a move.

My move had felt a lot stronger this morning when it was just a spark in my mind. Now that I was actually going through with it...I wasn't sure about this whole thing. I held a mint-green box of Death by Chocolate pastries in my hand and stared up at the Wright Construction building.

Sure, it held my namesake on the building, and I'd been there a million times before, but that didn't make it any easier. There were a million possibilities of someone I knew seeing me taking these upstairs.

And I was suddenly nervous and self-conscious. Not about me or David, but about what other people would think. I wished I could tie up other people's expectations in a bow, hide them away, and never consider them again, but that wasn't me.

With a deep breath, I pushed through the front door. My black Nikes squeaked across the recently waxed floor as I moved toward the elevators. One was mercifully empty when it dinged open for me. I pressed the button for the second to top floor, as the top floor was occupied by a fancy restaurant Wright used for parties, and zipped upward.

I held my breath as I watched the numbers tick up steadily faster. And released it when it opened on David's floor without a stop. Benefit of coming over before five. No one was trying to sneak out early quite yet.

David's floor was reserved for senior faculty. Like Morgan and Austin. It was quieter than some of the lower floors, but I knew how much work got done up here. I scampered past Austin's open office door. Then, I felt like an idiot when I realized it was empty. So was David's and Morgan's.

Oh…well, damn.

Guessed I should have called ahead to make sure he was even *in* the office. Though I didn't know where else he would be. He was a workaholic, just like Morgan. They both stayed after hours and showed up on weekends and disappeared to offices all over the country to take care of matters. So…where were they now?

I heard voices from the conference room and braced myself for the disaster I was about to walk into. I should turn around. Just walk back out from where I'd come from. But I didn't. I knocked.

The voices quieted, and then Morgan's face appeared. "Hey, Sut!"

"Hey, Mor."

Her eyes darted to my box. "Did you bring me treats?"

"Am I that nice?"

"Hmm...no," she conceded.

She pushed the door all the way open to reveal the conference room beyond in which Jensen, Austin, Landon, and David were all congregated. *Fucking wonderful.*

"Secret family meeting, and I wasn't invited?"

"You were working," Morgan said. "Plus, it's Wright shit. You don't care."

"Jensen and Landon don't work for Wright anymore," I pointed out.

"True. Why are you here?" Morgan asked with a smirk.

"I'm on the board," Jensen offered with a shrug.

Landon rolled his eyes. "I didn't want to be invited. I came over to talk about the golf course."

"I wouldn't have even brought it up, but I spoke with our lawyers about the Van Pelts. He thinks we might have to appear in New York if deliberations continue any longer," Jensen said.

"Oh," I said. "That's shitty. Right before your wedding."

"He'll let them keep our money before he messes up his big day," Morgan joked.

"Emery would murder me."

"Fact," Landon said under his breath.

"So…what are you doing here?" Morgan asked, batting her eyelashes at me, all innocent-like.

I dropped the box of sweets on the conference table. "I just came by to, uh…" I glanced around the room and then finally landed on David, who hadn't said anything since I walked in. He dutifully stood by while my family did their own thing. "Can I talk to you?"

"Sure."

He pushed his chair out, and I hurried out of the conference room before my family could butt their noses in. For sure they would. It was a matter of *when*, not if. This was why Morgan hadn't told anyone she was talking to Patrick in the first place. Having three older brothers in your business was anything but fun. Morgan at least was pretty good about it. Though she was cynical, and that sometimes made her…difficult. My whole family was, to be fair.

"What's up?" David asked.

I'd moved down the hallway some, away from the conference room where I was sure someone was trying to listen in on our conversation.

"Well…I brought you a box of sweets." I laughed. "Though…I guess…they'll probably be gone before you get back in there."

"That's okay. Just means I have to come by the bakery again."

"You should. I've been working on making these chocolate-and-strawberry cupcakes with Kimber, and I'm not bragging, but they might be the best thing I've ever made."

"I'll have to try them."

"I didn't really have a plan when I came over here and didn't expect my entire family to be here either. Kind of threw me off."

David smiled at my rambling. He looked the same way he had on Friday night right before he kissed me. My heart melted again.

"I missed you," he said before I could open my mouth again.

My cheeks heated. "It was kind of a lonely weekend."

"I wasn't sure if I'd…overstepped."

I shook my head and bit my bottom lip.

"Then, maybe we should do it again?" he suggested.

"I'd like that."

"Friday again?"

"I'll have to see if Jen is free."

"I'll plan for it then."

"Oh, wait," I said as it hit me. "I can't."

He laughed. "Are you already bailing? This is quicker than the last time."

"Hey now! That was…unfortunate. Different circumstances. This is because my cousins are flying in from Vancouver for the weekend. They're bringing my aunt, and I've never met her. We're having a thing. You could come by."

"Right. Morgan mentioned something about that. I kind of zoned out when she talked about it."

He boldly reached out and took my hand in his. My body turned to Jell-O at his touch. My knees going weak and my brain short-circuiting.

"I'd like to do that."

"Do…what?" I muttered, lost in his eyes, which were nearly green to match his button-up today.

"The party for your cousins."

"Right…right," I said, snapping out of it. "That sounds great."

"But I still want that date."

"Me, too," I admitted.

I was uncertain of how I'd gotten to this place where I was comfortable with going on a date…yet I was happy that it was happening. The best I could do was not second-guess it. And, as I stared into David's eyes, it was hard to feel anything other than sure about this.

Ten

David

I wasn't surprised that the welcome dinner for the Wright cousins was at La Sirena. It was Morgan's favorite restaurant in town, and she'd persuaded me several times to go there for work-related events. No matter that we had a restaurant on the top of our building for that exact purpose. This was what she wanted, so this was what she got.

Not that I expressly disagreed with her. The food was unbelievable. Latin fusion with a twist. Plus, the cocktails were out of this world.

Mostly, I was wondering why I was showing up for this thing at all. I'd met Jordan and Julian Wright last year when they showed up for Christmas to be with their dad. I wasn't a Wright though and didn't think I needed to meet their mother. But Morgan had invited me…and then Sutton. Well, I couldn't deny her anything.

That was how I ended up at a Wright family event as the only person not expressly family. The most I'd done was share a quick kiss with the youngest Wright, which had been playing on repeat in my mind. It had taken all my self-control not to kiss her again inside Wright Construction when she showed up after she got out of the bakery earlier this week.

I entered La Sirena and walked around the corner to the private wine room that Morgan had reserved. I pushed through the door, and my eyes found Sutton across the room. She had a glass of sangria in her hand and was shaking her head at Austin. Morgan and Jensen were speaking to their cousins and aunt while Landon and Patrick held court with the women— Emery, Heidi, and Julia.

Sutton's eyes twitched to the open door, landing on my face. A smile crept onto her lips, and her entire demeanor seemed to shift when I entered the room. As if she had just been getting by, and now, she was blossoming in the sunshine.

I nodded my head at Morgan before sauntering over to Sutton. "Hey," I said with a smile of my own. "You look great."

And she did. A flowy navy-blue dress with pink-and-white flowers, which tied up around her neck and waist. Her hair was curled at the ends, and she had on a dusting of sparkly makeup. She was practically glowing.

"Thanks. Annie and I went shopping this afternoon. She's a bundle of nerves about starting med school. So, all she does is shop."

"I'd probably be nervous, too." I turned to Austin and held my hand out. "Hey, man."

He shook a little harder than normal. "Hey." He tilted his head toward the bar. "Want to go get a drink?"

"Austin, you're not drinking!" Sutton hissed.

He held up his hands. "I was going to walk David to get a drink, Sut. I'm perfectly happy with my water."

I could read the deeper meaning behind his words. I was pretty sure Austin had been gearing up to this conversation all week. Morgan had probably kept it from happening at work. Better to get it over with.

"Yeah. A drink would be great." I gently touched Sutton's arm. "We'll be right back."

She nodded and then nervously glanced between us.

Austin and I moved across the small room and back out to the main bar. He leaned against the bar and appreciatively eyed all the liquors before averting his gaze. A black bartender with coily curls, wearing a red flannel shirt, came by, and I ordered a Texas Honey cocktail. She winked at me in response and began to pour the bourbon concoction.

"So...you and Sutton?" Austin finally said.

"Yep."

"When did that happen?"

"Recently."

"Are you sure that y'all should be dating?"

I looked him dead in the eye. "If she thinks she's ready, then she's ready. I would never pressure her to do more than she's comfortable with. All of this is up to her."

"Good. She's been through the wringer. She's strong, but I worry about her. We all do."

"I know you do. I was there the day Maverick died," I reminded him. "I remember what she was like before and what she was like after. Maybe not like you all do, but I can see the difference. I don't ever want to see her that unhappy ever again."

The bartender slid my drink to me, and I took a sip to steady myself.

"Me either," Austin agreed. "Look, I'm her big brother. I can't help it if I want to beat the shit out of you for thinking about touching my sister."

"Probably doesn't help that your best friend is now dating Morgan."

He rolled his eyes. "Don't even get me started."

"I kind of expected this from you anyway."

"Yeah?" he asked. "Well, just know that, if you hurt her, I'll kill you."

"Got it," I said with a laugh.

We shook hands, and Austin smiled. He was serious about how he'd react if I hurt Sutton, but I had no intention of ever doing that. Or at least...I hoped so.

"Come on. Let's go meet this aunt of mine. Pretty weird to have a new aunt after I'm thirty."

"I could see that. Family is always a bit crazy. New family is definitely so."

Sutton appeared at my elbow once we were back in the room. "What was that about?" she whispered.

"Nothing. Just getting the third degree from your brother."

She groaned. "Oh God, I was worried about that."

"It's fine. It was expected. We're good."

"But it's so embarrassing. We're not even..." She trailed off. "I don't know."

"And that's totally fine with me."

"Still...stupid, nosy brothers. No wonder Morgan was secretive," she muttered. "Whatever. I should probably introduce you to my aunt."

She gestured for me to follow her, and we walked over to where Morgan and Jensen were chatting with a woman in her mid-fifties with graying-blonde hair and a soft smile. She wore a modest pink blouse and long black skirt that made her seem even meeker.

"Helene," Sutton said, "this is the Wright Construction CFO, David Calloway."

"Pleased to meet you," I said, holding out my hand.

"Delighted," she said. Her handshake was as light as her voice. "I'm so happy to be home. It's the first time back since I moved to Vancouver."

"We're glad to bring you home," Julian, the younger of the two cousins, said. He put a protective hand on his mother's arm.

Jordan's face was pinched, and he said nothing, just nodded. His eyes kept darting around the room and then back to his mother, as if he couldn't quite believe they were there. Or maybe he wanted to get her out of there, away from so many people. He was stern, and I was certain he wanted to bolt. Strange, considering he was here on vacation.

"How is Vancouver this time of year?" I asked.

"Well, it's not Texas," Julian said with a laugh. "We're not used to this heat."

"It's the wind and sand you have to get used to," I assured him. "After San Francisco summers, I thought I'd never acclimate to Lubbock, but I'm coming around to it."

"You love the evenings," Sutton said. "Admit it. It's gorgeous. And nothing can beat a Lubbock sunset."

"Oh, I've missed the sunsets," Helene said.

"Fine. I enjoy the sunsets and the evenings," I conceded to Sutton with a grin.

She blushed slightly at the look and turned back to her aunt.

"Aren't you two adorable?"

Morgan laughed and then covered it with a cough. "Why don't we grab our seats? I, for one, am starving."

Sutton hid her pink cheeks from everyone as they maneuvered around us. My eyes followed the rest of her family. Julian kept his hand on the small of his mom's back. Jordan walked stiffly behind them. Helene appeared oblivious to the entire thing, but there was something about her. Something that I couldn't quite place. I didn't know what it was though.

"I didn't quite realize how this would look before you got here," Sutton said as she gestured for us to sit at the end of the table.

"Like we're dating?" I asked.

She nodded.

"Morgan did invite me before you did. I was already planning to attend."

"But still."

She was right, of course. It did look like we were dating. And it put pressure on her when she didn't need it. Or when she wasn't ready. She had freaked out that first night when she thought we were going on a date. I wouldn't blame her if she started getting spooked in this situation.

"Do you want me to go?"

"What?" she asked with round eyes as she took her seat across from Landon and Heidi. "No, of course not."

"Okay. But I would."

"That's not what I want."

I moved my hand under the table and clasped hers in mine. Her hand was warm and so fucking inviting. She squeezed gently on my hand before surreptitiously releasing it.

I still wasn't sure where that left us. But I was more than ready to find out.

It was a couple of hours later before we finished off our meals and were finally leaving La Sirena. It was near to closing. I was sure the staff was happy to see us gone for the night, but they couldn't deny the generous tip we'd left.

I fell into step beside Sutton as we descended on the parking lot. I'd parked next to her Audi. She stepped carefully across the gravel in her heels before reaching her door. She turned around to face me as her siblings' cars all vanished from the parking lot, leaving us all alone.

"I had a great night," I told her. "I'm glad I stayed."

"Me, too. David, I want you to know that I'm not embarrassed to be seen with you or for my aunt to think we're a couple. I don't know what we're doing just yet. Can we kind of go with the flow?"

"Absolutely," I said, taking a step closer to her.

She stared up at me through thick black lashes. "I couldn't get Jen to watch Jason this weekend or next. She's busy."

"That's okay," I told her.

"We could always stay in," she sputtered and covered her mouth. "That's…not what I meant. What I meant is…"

"You need to stay in to watch Jason for the night." I took another step closer.

She nodded and leaned forward, as if we were magnets.

"We could have a night in with him if you'd like. I don't mind."

"Are you sure?"

"I adore your son, Sutton. I don't mind anything that's easier for you."

She smiled and then stood on her tiptoes. Her lips hovered in front of mine. Then, I grabbed her around the middle and dragged her against my body, pressing our lips together. She moaned into the kiss, and I opened her mouth to mine, thoroughly tasting her. I lost all time in that parking lot. I hoped I never found it again.

Eleven

David

"Sorry it's so early," Sutton said when I appeared at the house.

Jason usually passed out in the early evening, so I'd shown up with enough time for the three of us to be together. Being a single parent couldn't be easy on her. I knew that she'd gotten Jenny so that she could still have a semblance of a life. Also, it helped now that she was working. But it didn't seem fair to always make her get a sitter when I used to babysit Jason. He was a great kid.

"Don't worry about it. Anything I can help with?"

"Uh...there's sunscreen in that drawer. We're all going to need it." She hurried down the hallway and collected Jason from his playroom.

Jason laughed when he saw me and tried to hand me the baby doll and a container of syrup. "Yes! Park!"

"Thanks, bud," I said, taking the doll from his hand and staring at the syrup perplexed. "Why do you have syrup?"

"Don't ask questions," Sutton called back. "Modern parenting."

I laughed and took the offered syrup bottle, too. Then, he found a stray truck and gave that to me, too.

"Just what I wanted." I dropped all of them back into a container and grabbed the sunscreen out of the drawer. "Are you ready to go to the park?"

He threw both his hands up and yelled, "Yes!"

"Sunscreen first, Jay," Sutton said.

I tossed it to her, and she thoroughly lathered Jason in the sunscreen while he complained intensely about it.

"You, too." She tossed the bottle back to me. "No sunburns all around."

I laughed but coated my neck, arms, and face as well. She busied herself with filling up a stroller with everything we could possibly need in a quick trip to the park, which, admittedly, was a shit-ton of stuff. I had underestimated how much a toddler needed on one trip out of the house.

Sutton buckled Jason in the stroller and then pushed it onto the sidewalk. She plopped a giant-rimmed floppy hat on the top of her head and smiled at me. "It's blistering out here."

"Texas summers. Why don't you let me push?"

"All right," she said softly, stepping to the side.

Jason munched on organic white cheddar puffs and pretzels as we walked side by side down Sutton's street on the south side of town. It was a newer development, so it didn't have the shade of some of the older neighborhoods. But there was a park less than a half-mile from the house with a lake, gravel walking trail, playground, and picnic tables. Kind of a dream when you had a toddler.

"I love your neighborhood," I said. "It's perfect."

"Yeah. Jason loves it here. He has friends on our block. Just hard...being in the house sometimes."

I nodded. "I could see that."

"We come to the park a lot actually. Better than sitting around inside. It's why he's so tan," she said with a smile. "That, and the swimming pool. Kid *loves* the swimming pool."

"You have one for the neighborhood?"

"Yep. Best part of the outrageous HOA fee I pay," she said with an eye roll.

I laughed. I knew what that was like. I'd seen some of the most exorbitant costs for housing and upkeep ever. Her yearly HOA was probably less than the *monthly* fee for where my parents lived.

"Okay, buddy," Sutton said once we reached the mostly empty park.

She unbuckled him. He immediately raced toward the swings. We left the stroller parked nearby and followed him.

"Push!" Jason pointed at the swing.

"I gotcha," I said, picking him up and placing him in the bucket swing.

He started rocking back and forth, as if he could propel himself into action. I moved around behind him, gently pushing him in the swing.

Sutton sank into the swing next to Jason's and stared up at us with big eyes. She looked like she'd gotten all gooey and was trying not to melt into a puddle on the floor.

"I can get you, too."

She raised an eyebrow. But then I switched to her seat, pulled the swing back, and released to get her going. She laughed and kicked her feet to continue her ascent. I alternated between a gentle push for Jason and a bigger push for Sutton. Jason giggled and pointed at his mom. Sutton was laughing, too. Throwing her head back and arching her back to get more air. She looked so…free.

All the tension rolled off her shoulders, and it was easy to see that she was only twenty-four years old. She'd lost so much. She'd endured. And here she was, still as beautiful as ever, not falling apart because of it.

"Watch out," she said.

And then she vaulted off the swing and into the air before landing uneasily on her feet. Then, she rolled and lay down in the grass in a fit of laughter.

"Oh my God, I haven't done that in forever."

"Excellent dismount."

"Ha!" she said. "Not my best. I could probably pull out a back handspring right now if I wanted."

"I'd throw my back out if I tried that."

"Fifteen years of gymnastics and cheerleading, and I still probably would." She moved over to Jason, tugging him out of the swing. "Let's do the slide."

"Slide," he said, racing toward the jungle gym.

There was a smaller slide on the side of the big construction that he only had to climb up two steps to get to. And though he kept eyeing the big slide, he hurried to the small slide.

"Mom! Mommy!"

"You got it! Let's see," Sutton encouraged.

She was sitting at the end of the slide, waiting for him to slide down. He pushed his way down, and then she scooped him up and swung him in a circle.

"Yay! Good job."

"Again!" he crooned and then ran back to the stairs.

We watched him together for at least five million slides. Every single one of them, he insisted that we watch him and applaud his mad skills. It was surprisingly entertaining, all things considered.

Jason was sliding down his five millionth and one time when Sutton looked like she was about to fall over. It was at that time when one of Jason's friends showed up, and he hurried over to play with the girl. Sutton nodded at the dad carting his daughter around and then plopped down onto a bench.

"I'm so glad he has friends," she said. "Only time I get a reprieve."

"He's such a great kid."

"He is." She smiled with her eyes glued to Jason like a hawk. "Do you still keep up with your friends from home? The ones who you got in trouble with?"

"Oh," I said, taken off guard. "No, not really. I'd known them my whole life, but I only really liked Court. He was kind of a jackass, but at least he was an honest one."

"I can understand that."

"The rest were...cling-ons. They wanted to be Court or close to him. He had that charisma, you know? Our families were like peas in a pod, so we always got along. I never had to work for his time."

"Ah, yes. Jensen has that charisma."

I nodded. "Definitely. I'm honestly surprised Katherine isn't marrying Court's brother. I thought that was the obvious choice."

"Did they date?"

"Nah. But they were best friends. We all thought it would happen. But, no...she's marrying someone else. Guy's kind of a douche actually."

She laughed. "Sounds like you know a lot of them."

"Yeah. That's fair."

"Well, all of this sounds better than my friends."

"Annie and Jenny are amazing."

"Yes," she agreed. A sadness cloaked her face for a moment. "But all my college friends kind of disappeared. They called and came by when Mav first died, but I guess, when it became clear that I wasn't going to bounce back right away, they all slowly moved away and never spoke to me again." She sighed. "Sorry to keep bringing him up."

"First, they don't sound like real friends."

"They weren't. I know that now. Hard way to find out who really matters."

I reached out and laced my fingers through Sutton's. She glanced down at our hands and flushed.

"Second, you never have to apologize to me about Maverick."

"It's just...awkward. Isn't it?"

"He was your husband. I'm not here to shame you into never thinking about him again. Frankly, it'd be a little weird if you never thought about him."

"Really?" she whispered. "Everyone else treats me like a pariah every time I bring him up. Like it'd be easier for me if I just forgot about him."

"You're not a pariah, and you don't have to forget him. For Jason's sake, I hope that you don't."

Sutton's eyes snapped back to her son playing in the sandbox with the other toddler. "I wish he didn't have to grow up without his father. I know what that's like, and it sucks."

"You're doing a great job. You know that, right? You're a great mom."

Tears welled in the corners of her eyes. "Thanks. That's, like...the best compliment anyone could give me."

I kissed her forehead and helped her up. "Come on. Let's get out of this oppressive sun. There's pizza and a movie with your name on it back at the house."

"You're making pizza?"

"Yeah, no. But I know how to order one for delivery."

She giggled, swiping the lingering tear from her eye. "Even better. No dishes."

We wrangled Jason, and heedless of the sand he was now covered in, I threw him onto my shoulders for the walk back to the house. Sutton pushed the stroller but kept glancing up at the two of us as if we were a mirage...or a memory.

Twelve

Sutton

As soon as we were home, I disappeared into the bathroom with Jason. He needed a bath after playing in the sandbox, but I'd be lying if I said I didn't need a moment to regroup. Watching David with Jason was…heart-wrenching. And wonderful.

All the things Maverick was missing.

All the things David was getting instead.

It was wrong to compare them. Maverick and David were nothing alike. Maverick had been funny and silly and always an adventure. David was more serious. He had this look in his eyes that said he'd been through shit, but I could never tell if I was just projecting.

Plus, Maverick would always be what once was, and I couldn't compare David to a ghost. They weren't the same. I didn't want them to be. But, sometimes, it was hard seeing David in Mav's place.

Taking that extra minute to wash the sand off of Jason was enough for me to feel sane again. I changed him into his new favorite pajamas that said *Future President* and hauled him back out to the living room.

"Why don't you pick out a movie?" I told him.

He raced to the movie cabinet and began pulling every single movie we owned off the shelves.

"Pizza should be here in fifteen minutes," David said.

"Great."

Jason picked *Trolls*, of course. I popped the movie into the player and set Jason down on the couch. David sat next to him, and I took the other spot.

"Bet this is exactly what you were expecting when you asked me out."

"I mean...I was kind of expecting *Thor*. Abs and all," he joked.

"Ha-ha. You're so funny."

He wickedly grinned at me before slinging his arm across the back of the couch and pulling all of us closer together. *Magical.*

———

By the time pizza arrived, David was as deeply engrossed in the movie as Jason was. I rolled my eyes at the pair of them and got up to get food. We ate our pizza on paper plates in the living room and sang along to the songs until Jason's eyes were drooping. Eventually, he lost the fight and fell into a deep sleep, still sitting between us.

David swept Jason's thick hair off his forehead. "I'll carry him into his room if you get the door."

With practiced ease, he carefully hoisted Jason into his hands. I walked in front of him and opened the door to Jason's bedroom, tugging back the covers to his toddler bed. David gently laid him down on the mattress and tucked him in. His little head lolled to the side. He was completely out of it.

"Guess all of that time in the sun wore him out," I whispered. "Usually, bedtime is an ordeal."

David nodded. "Seems so."

I bent down and kissed Jason on the forehead before quietly exiting the bedroom with David. I peeked inside one more time to get another look at my slumbering boy before walking back to the living room with David. Where we were finally…finally alone.

Our eyes met, and my heart stuttered at that look. Desire coiled through me—as hot as it was unexpected.

I wanted this man.

That much was so obvious to me.

Yet…I hesitated. I awkwardly stood there, staring up at him, like I'd never been intimate with anyone before. The two-year-old in the other room proved that wrong. But, of course, he was also one of the main reasons I hadn't been with anyone else in over a year.

I hated this part. This pause. This inaction. This second-guessing.

Even if it was perfectly reasonable for me to question moving forward.

As if David could see what was racing through my mind, he reached down and picked up the remote. "Do you still want to finish the movie?"

I laughed, releasing some of that tension. "Do you know how many times I've seen this?"

"At least a hundred."

"At least."

David flipped the TV off, bathing us in darkness, except for the soft light coming from the side table. I chewed on my bottom lip.

"Do you...want a drink?"

He shook his head. "I'm all right."

Then, he stepped across the room. His fingers pushed up into my dark hair and tilted my face up to look at him. My pulse accelerated, and both fear and excitement struck me like lightning.

"Are you all right?"

When I looked up into those golden eyes, I lost all thought, all doubt. I just nodded. And he kissed me.

I exhaled softly as a groan escaped me. He tasted delicious and utterly, undeniably wonderful. Our lips melded together. He opened my mouth on a sigh. Our tongues volleyed, meeting and touching and tempting. We stayed like that, lost in a perfect kiss, until he dragged my bottom lip between his teeth and then moved to kiss down my neck.

Goose bumps erupted on my skin. I felt as hot as the Texas summer. My body couldn't seem to keep up with the sensations it had been deprived of. Everything was so intense, so much. I wanted to dive into a cold pool, into this feeling of exquisite rightness.

I arched my body against his chest. His hands slipped down my back, digging into the muscles as he scooped his way down, down, down. He wasn't tentative or questioning when he grabbed my ass, and

I didn't try to stop him. If anything, my moan and thrust against him only indicated the opposite.

I was aching for more.

Aching to feel again.

He bent forward, capturing my lips again. Then, he grasped my outer thighs and lifted me into the air. A breath loosed from my mouth as I threw my arms around his neck and my legs around his waist.

I was now at eye-level, which, with his considerable height, never happened. I could see the molten-gold ring around his eyes and the little flecks of green that threatened to take over when he wore the color. My body pulsed against him. I was sure he could feel it.

His enthusiastic smile at my reaction was enough to say that he didn't care. Not one ounce.

My lips found his, and he walked us back to the couch where he took a seat with me straddling him. My dress was hiked up to the tops of my thighs, and his hands explored the exposed flesh. Getting intimately acquainted with every inch of my skin. Every sweep of his hands became bolder and bolder until they strayed up to the hem of my pink thong.

My body jerked in response, and that was when I felt him through his khaki shorts. I gasped as desire shot through me like nothing before. His hardened dick was so…inviting. It would be so easy to just strip him out of those shorts and find sweet relief. Quench that throbbing need.

But I reined myself in. I wasn't even on the pill. I didn't need another whoops. One was enough.

"Fuck," David groaned against my mouth. "You're…fuck."

"I know," I whispered.

"Are you…do you…want to keep going?" he asked.

My heart melted for this man. He didn't just take. He could. I would have let him. But…he still wanted to make sure I was okay. Through all of this, he was worried about me. I could just kiss him.

And I did.

"Yes," I murmured against his lips.

His arms tightened around my body, squeezing me close once before laying my body back on the couch. I inhaled deeply as he started at my knee and began kissing his way down my inner thigh. He spread my legs a little further before brushing his nose against the satin of my thong.

I groaned, quite ready to throw my underwear off and toss them at him. But he was secure in taking his time. Slipping a finger under the material and swishing it down between the folds. He grinned up at me when he felt how wet I already was. He teased me with my own wetness before dragging my thong down my legs.

He wet his fingers and then circled my clit until I was thrashing. I was whimpering and practically begging for more by the time he inserted two fingers inside me.

"Oh," I gasped.

I wanted more, but dear Lord, this was…so good.

He pumped in and out of me a few times, bringing me to the edge and then releasing me. When I thought I couldn't take any more, his tongue replaced his thumb, still working my clit. My head whipped backward, and I arched off the couch. My entire body tensed, centering in my core, as if it were building pressure.

Then, I stepped on the land mine, and everything exploded. It shot out from my core, up through my chest, and all the way to my fingers and toes. I curled into myself and said frantically, "Oh my God. Oh my God. Oh my fucking God."

Finally, my eyes opened, and I stared at a rather satisfied David.

"God, you're beautiful."

I laughed softly. "Wow."

Wow was the only word in my vocabulary at the moment. I was running on a total high. That was the best orgasm I'd had in a long, long time. My body felt like jelly. My mind was full of cotton balls. Everything was so slow and so good.

David pulled my dress back over my lower half and leaned up to kiss my cheek. "I really want to have sex with you," he admitted in a moment of perfect honesty.

And, in that same second, reality smacked me in the face.

Sex.

Oh, man.

I wasn't ready for that. I…I wasn't even sure if I was ready for what had just happened. It had been perfect, yet now, I was wondering if it was too soon. We'd only been talking for a couple of weeks. Sure, he was great with Jason, but was I ready for Jason to have a real father figure in his life? Was it too soon?

Stupid brain. I wished it would shut up for once.

"I'm not…not ready," I finally told him.

David leaned his forehead into my shoulder. "Okay."

"You sure?"

"I'm just going to need a cold shower," he said on a hoarse laugh. "Your orgasm nearly did me in."

My face turned the color of a tomato. "Oh."

He gently kissed my cheek. "It's okay. If you're not ready, you're not ready."

I kind of adored him for that comment. He was giving me all the space I wanted. And, apparently, an epic orgasm…and I hoped I'd soon be ready for a second one of those. He drew me close to him one more time, and then I wistfully watched him leave.

Jason slumbered in another bedroom, but the quiet creeped me out. I wrapped my arms around myself as the ghosts of the past threatened me. It was much easier when there were other people around. When I didn't have to remember what it had been like when the silences were filled or realize I was forgetting the sound of Maverick's voice.

For once, I hoped the amazing evening would block out the nightmares.

Thirteen

Sutton

Jason and I were driving home from church the next morning when I noticed a big red pickup truck in my driveway. My stomach clenched. So, *that* was what those missed calls had been about.

"Great," I grumbled.

That was definitely Maverick's parents' truck. They lived outside of Lubbock and must have driven in when they hadn't heard from me in a while. I hadn't thought much of it because I was spending more time with David.

But, this morning, I hadn't even avoided their calls. I'd been in church. Admittedly, Jason and I hadn't been particularly devout since Mav passed. But, considering the escapades from last night, I'd thought it would be good to put in the effort. Now, I was regretting doing anything if this was the result.

I parked my Audi in the garage and moved to the backseat to get Jason out of his car seat. Maverick's parents—Ray and Linda—waited on the front step when I finally got him inside.

"What a surprise!" I said, mustering some enthusiasm.

"Sutton, so good to see you," Linda said. She kissed my cheek and then bustled into the house. "Where's my grandson?"

"Grandma!" Jason cried.

He raced toward her, and she scooped him up into her arms.

"Hey, come on in," I said to Ray.

He tipped his cowboy hat at me and entered the house. I looked to the ceiling for patience and then closed the door.

"What brings y'all into the big city?" I joked.

"We tried to call," Linda said.

"Right. We were in church."

"You were in church all week? I was trying to find a time to come see my grandbaby."

"Well, I got a new job recently, so I've been kind of busy."

"A job?" Linda asked. "What have you been doing? Who has been looking out for Jason? You know, I can always come into town every morning and watch him for you."

"Yep. I'm working at a bakery downtown. Jenny has been watching him. She's the nanny I got last year. She's been with him a long time. He's into a routine now. I don't think you need to come into town to watch him."

"Just because you have money doesn't mean you should waste it."

I held my breath to keep from snapping back at her. As if that wasn't an argument she'd brought up with me nearly every time that I met her. Especially when Maverick had decided to change his last name to Wright. It hadn't even been my suggestion. He'd done it all on his own and surprised me.

"Trying to keep the amount of change in Jason's life to a minimum," I told her instead.

"Of course, of course. You're his mother."

I walked past them toward the kitchen to keep from rolling my eyes. "Did y'all want a drink? Water, Coke, sweet tea?"

"Tea for me," Ray said.

"Same," Linda said.

I took a breather in the kitchen, preparing the drinks as slow as possible. I liked Maverick's parents. We usually got along. But Maverick was their only child. After he'd passed, things had changed between us. I became their daughter, and at the same time, I wasn't good enough to replace Maverick. It was messy, and I tried to tolerate Linda's nagging. She meant well, and I was glad she wanted a real relationship with Jason. It meant a lot to me and to him.

After adding lemons to their drinks, I carried them out into the living room.

"Mommy, where David?" Jason asked from the floor where he was playing with his truck.

I froze in the middle of the living room, a full glass of sweet tea in each hand. I couldn't believe the words that had come out of my son's mouth. "What, honey?"

"David," he repeated, rolling a W instead of a V.

"Who's David?" Linda asked Jason.

"My friend." He lost the R entirely.

Linda's eyes widened, and she looked up at me. "Is this friend the reason you haven't been answering our phone calls?"

"No. David works at Wright Construction."

"And...you two are?"

I set down the glasses of sweet tea on coasters. I had not prepared myself well enough for this conversation. My hands were shaking. My stomach was in knots. I suddenly felt sick. It wasn't like David and I were hiding what we were doing, but I hadn't thought about having this conversation with Maverick's parents. It was complicated enough without that added in.

"Seeing each other," I finally got out.

"I see," Linda muttered. She stood from where she'd been hanging out with Jason.

"Mommy?" he asked.

I smiled down at him. "David isn't here right now. Why don't you play with your blocks while Grandma, Grandpa, and I talk?"

He never argued with uninterrupted playtime. I straightened again and tried to steel myself for this upcoming conversation with my in-laws. It wasn't going to be pretty.

"This is a new thing. David and I started seeing each other recently. Jason knows David because he used to babysit for me before I got Jenny. They actually are friends."

"Dating already," Linda said, fanning herself.

"It's been over a year."

"Replacing Maverick in a year. I can't fathom it."

"I'm not replacing him. But I'm young. I can't mourn eternally."

"Maverick is still gone. Our baby." She clutched Ray's hand, who remained silent through the exchange.

"I know. I miss him," I said softly. "This isn't easy for me. And I'm not taking it lightly."

"Bringing another man into Jason's life is very troubling," Linda said. "It can be confusing, especially this soon. If you just started seeing each other and are affectionate around him, imagine what he must be thinking. He's so young and impressionable. What happens if this falls through? Are you going to bring a cycle of men into my grandson's life?"

I wanted to erupt on her, but I kept my cool. I knew where she was coming from, and...I was concerned about Jason's reaction to me dating again. But I was in no way bringing a cycle of men into his life. I hadn't even been ready to date a month ago. I was hardly going to parade people in front of my son. The only reason I'd brought David around him was because they already knew each other. David and Jason had an established relationship. I wasn't acting reckless.

"I'm not going to start dating a bunch of people. I only just started seeing David. All of this is new."

"And about that...how could you bring him around Jason when you just got together?"

"I already told you that David used to babysit."

"It's entirely different, and you know it."

"Look, I know what's best for my son."

Linda huffed. "That might be true, but sometimes, we don't always think through our actions. We're looking out for you and Jason. That's our main concern."

"Thank you for your concern. But Jason and I are just fine."

"Honestly, Sutton, I think you're a little blind to this. Have you considered that?" Linda asked. "If you knew this decision was best, then would you have avoided us? Wouldn't you have told us the truth?" She almost seemed near to tears.

My heart shifted from anger to worry. *Am I dismissing her too easily? Had I held this information back from her for a reason?*

I'd thought I was doing it because I didn't know how they would react to me seeing someone else. I hadn't really considered their thoughts on Jason. He was my son and my first priority.

I glanced over at him still playing in the living room. I didn't want to confuse him. Maybe having David over…or dating at all would be confusing. *Am I fucking up my son without even meaning to?*

Christ, this mom stuff was the hardest job on the planet. I needed to see my therapist. I needed to…stop thinking about all of this. Of course Maverick's parents would say these things. It was okay…maybe…probably.

"You know, why don't we take Jason for the afternoon?" Ray suggested, finally speaking up. "We've missed the little tyke. And you look like you could use a break."

I smiled wanly at him. "Y'all don't have to do that."

"We want to," he insisted.

Ray moved into the living room and bent down to talk to Jason, who squealed with delight at the prospect of going out with his grandma and grandpa.

Linda rested her hand on my arm. "Maverick has only been gone a year."

"I know," I whispered.

"He left behind the best gift you could ever have. And that means this isn't all about you anymore. You need to decide if this is what's really best for Jason...or just for you."

Jason gave me a big hug and kiss and then left the house with his grandparents. Linda gave me one more meaningful look before departing and leaving me alone in this big-ass house.

"Oh God," I whispered as Maverick's presence seemed to permeate through everything.

Maybe she was right.

Fourteen

David

"I don't know how many other ways to tell you. I'm not coming home," I told Katherine on the phone.

She'd called a half hour ago to try to convince me to come back, but that was out of the question. She knew I wasn't coming back.

"David, be reasonable," Katherine said.

"This is me being reasonable. I'm on the phone with you. I don't have to be. I have other things going on in my life."

"Will you talk to Mom?"

"No," I said emphatically.

"She'd really love to hear from you. It's been so long."

"I know that you're on their side, Ren, but I'm not."

Katherine exhaled noisily in frustration. "Have you at least decided about the wedding?"

"Are you actually going through with it?" I joked.

Her response was feral. "I don't talk about your poor life choices. You don't have to talk about mine."

"Fine, fine."

I could practically see her eye roll. "So, just come home already. Fuck."

"You know that's not happening. Why must you keep bothering me about it? I have a new job. I'm happy here. I'm seeing someone. Don't drag me back into your shit."

"You're seeing someone?" Katherine asked. Her voice shot up an octave. "That's new."

Well, fuck. Now, I'd done it.

"Yes. It's very new."

"Details. I'm still a girl here."

"She's my boss's sister. She's younger than me. Younger than you actually."

"Robbing the cradle?"

"No," I said with a laugh. Talking about Sutton actually lightened my entire mood. It was so much easier to talk to Katherine about this than to discuss our parents. "No, she's definitely an adult. She has a two-year-old son."

"Whoa! Wait, hold up," Katherine said in disbelief. "You're dating a single mom?"

"Yeah," I said cautiously.

"That's crazy! I never would have pegged you as the type."

"What type is that?"

"God…not type. But I just didn't imagine you as a dad. It's super weird to think about. I still see you as you were in high school. Thinking of you with a kid…that's just…surprising. Are you really ready to be someone's *dad?*"

Dad.

Whoa.

Okay, so I hadn't thought about it in those terms. Yes, I wanted to date Sutton. Yes, I loved Jason. Yes, I knew they were a package deal. But the word *dad* had never really crossed my mind. And, with my fucked up past…it wasn't really a word I was comfortable with. I was not close to my father. Not by a long shot. My past was complicated. Adopting a kid…well, I knew that had a lot of its own difficulties.

I swallowed back the rising panic in my chest. I knew I was getting ahead of myself. It wasn't like I was going to marry Sutton tomorrow and pick up right where Maverick had left off. That was a horrible notion to even consider. She was hardly ready for a relationship. There was no way we were going to move into that route anytime soon.

But thinking about it was…not rational. I needed to shut down those insecurities. Because that was what it was…my own fears about my upbringing. And, if I wanted to see where this would go with Sutton, then I needed to give it a fair shot.

"You know what? That's really none of your concern," I finally said to Katherine.

"Okay. Fine. Whatever," she grumbled. "Maybe I can see you and meet this girlfriend of yours?"

No chance in hell.

"Maybe," I said instead.

My phone buzzed in my ear, and I pulled it away to glance at the text that had come in.

> *I hate doing this in text, but…I really don't think we're a good idea. It's not fair to Jason, and I have to make him my first*

*priority. I thought I was ready, but I'm not.
I'm really sorry.*

My heart stopped beating for a second, and I held my breath as I read and reread the text.

What the hell?

Where had this come from?

I just…

I had no idea how to even explain this text message.

Yesterday, we'd have an incredible day together. Everything had been great with Jason. Better than great even. Things had gotten heated, but I hadn't pressured her to do anything. She'd wanted what was happening.

And, now…

Now, we were through?

If she really wasn't ready, then okay.

But this…

Christ, this didn't sound like Sutton.

I didn't know what to think. Because I wanted to listen to her. I wanted to believe what she'd said. I wanted to hear her call for help and her cry of pain. If anything, I just wanted to be there for her. We didn't have to get physical if that was too fast.

But all of this because of Jason?

Something was wrong. I couldn't accept this explanation through a text message. She was hiding. She didn't want to confront me in person. I couldn't think that she would say the same thing if we came face-to-face. Maybe I was stretching, but that was my story, and I was sticking to it.

"David? Hello? Are you still there?" Katherine asked.

"I have to go. I'll talk to you later."

"Uh…okay. Everything okay?"

"Not sure. I have to take care of something."

"All right. Later then."

I said good-bye and then hung up the phone. My hands were shaking. I took a deep breath and then shook my hands out. It was perfectly reasonable for Sutton to feel upset after what had happened last night. I didn't want to think so, but that was ego, not logic.

Logically…that was probably her first sexual experience since her husband had died. That'd probably freaked her out. It had probably taken her a minute to come to that conclusion, and now, she was pumping the brakes.

I needed to talk to her and figure this out. Because we *could* figure this out.

I hastily pressed the button for her number and put my phone to my ear. It rang three times before abruptly ending. I cursed and tried again. No go. She was avoiding me.

Okay. Drastic measures.

Without a second thought, I grabbed the keys to my Ferrari and was out the door. It normally took me ten minutes to get to Sutton's house, but I was glad there weren't any cops out today. I broke every speed limit on the way over. The Ferrari was made for the long stretches where I could open up and blow past everyone else in sight.

I parked out front and dashed up the sidewalk to her front door. I didn't know if she was home, but it was as good of a place as any to try. I knocked on the front door and waited for someone to answer. I couldn't seem to stand still. I kept pacing back and forth in front of her door.

When she didn't answer, I knocked again. "Sutton? Are you in there? We should talk about this."

I waited a full minute before I heard the lock slide open. Sutton creaked the front door open and peered out. She looked like a different woman from last night. Her hair was in a topknot, she wasn't wearing any makeup, and she was in yoga pants and an old tank. I still thought she looked beautiful, but I hated that she was beating herself up.

"Hey," she muttered.

"Can I come in?"

"Actually…that's not such a good idea."

I ran a hand back through my hair. "You can't send me a text like that and expect me to just be okay with it."

Her eyes narrowed. "I think I can do precisely that."

"Yes," I said, blowing out a harsh breath. "You can. You can if you want to. But I thought we were on the same page. Are you okay? Did something happen?"

"No," she whispered. Then, she glanced off to the left. So, yes, something had happened. "I need to think about Jason here."

"What changed between last night and tonight?"

She paused before saying, "Nothing—I don't know—everything." She chewed on her bottom lip. "I thought I was ready to date, but I'm not. It's still too hard. I was married a year ago and happy. Now, I'm alone and miserable, and I don't know when that's going to change."

"I'm sorry. I can't imagine this is easy."

"It's not. And it's not easy for Jason either. Being intimate around him...even holding hands...I mean, what is he supposed to think?"

"We don't have to be," I assured her.

"I think you should leave," she whispered with no conviction.

"Sutton...please, if this is about sex, I'm okay with waiting."

She bloomed a bright red color. "No, it's not about sex. It's about Jason and...and me. Can you please go? I'm sorry."

"I don't want to leave you here right now. You look like you're having a mental breakdown. I could take you to get dinner, or I could bring you dinner if you want to stay in with Jason."

"Jason isn't home. He's with his grandparents."

A lightbulb flashed in my mind. His grandparents. That must be Maverick's parents, considering Sutton's parents were both deceased. That meant that she had spoken to Maverick's parents today. *Had they somehow found out about us? Were they upset? Projecting?*

"Did they say something?"

She choked on her next words. "I'm a mom, David. You don't have kids. You can't understand what kind of responsibility that is. I have to protect him. If I don't, who will? Can you understand that?"

I nodded numbly. She was really set on this. After a year of waiting for this moment, I had only gotten a few weeks with her. I'd second-guessed whether or not I wanted Jason long-term when I was on the phone with Katherine. And maybe she was right; I wasn't ready to be a dad. But it had only been such a short period of time. I was ready to be here for

111

Sutton if she needed me, and I could grow into the other responsibilities. I hated that she felt that she had to protect Jason from me when he and I had been so close before this.

"Sutton…"

She shook her head. "I'm sorry."

Then, she shut the door in my face, leaving me standing on her porch, feeling like a total idiot. If she didn't already have some fear about us, then Maverick's parents couldn't have gotten into her head. I thought it was reasonable to be afraid. I didn't think this would be easy or perfect overnight, but I'd been willing to try.

Now, she was going to throw it all away, and there was nothing I could do to change her mind.

Because she was right; Jason did come first.

And, if she felt it was better for me to not be near him, then by all means, I respected her decision.

But I didn't have to like it.

Fifteen

David

It had been a long time since I felt like this.

No matter what I did or said, I wasn't going to change Sutton's mind.

I didn't try to get her to answer the door again. That would be torture for her. She'd said her piece, and that was that. But it felt hollow.

And the thought that she didn't trust me with him was equally heartbreaking. He wasn't my kid, but I adored him. I wanted Sutton to trust me with him. I never expected that to happen overnight, but it'd been a year of me helping out with him. I hadn't realized that would change when we started dating.

My mind was a firestorm.

It burned through me relentlessly.

But there was nothing I could do. So, I did the only thing I knew how to do. I worked. I lost myself in paperwork and emails and contracts. It was the easiest way not to have to process what had happened.

I was always the first person in the office anyway, but I got in before the doors were even unlocked on Monday morning. It sucked because mysterious wet stuff we never saw in Texas was falling from the sky in a torrential downpour, and someone had forgotten a fucking umbrella. I fumbled with my keys until I got inside, turned off the security system, and went up to my office, soaked through. Really…just fucking great. When it rained, it poured.

I slopped my suit jacket onto a chair to dry, untucked my white button-up, and then pulled it off as well. When I was nearly undressed in my office was the moment Morgan stuck her head inside.

"David, you're in extra early…" Then, she stopped. "Well, isn't this awkward?"

"Hey, Mor. What? What's awkward?"

"I'm pretty sure Julia would file this under sexual harassment. So, I should probably tell you to put your clothes back on and get to work." Morgan snickered.

"Forgot the umbrella."

"Maybe keep an spare suit in the office next time."

"Roger that."

"Or air-dry them in the restroom?"

"Drying an Armani shirt with a hand dryer in the restroom is about the state of my life right now."

Morgan tried to rein in her laughter. "You look like a sad, wet dog. What happened to you?"

"Sutton," I told her.

Her laughter died out. "I thought things were going well."

"They were going well. Until she decided they weren't."

"I see." She sighed heavily. "I mean, I'm not going to say I'm surprised. I'm not surprised. But that doesn't mean I don't feel for you. Why don't we cut out early and get a beer? You can cry on my shoulder."

"Early?" I asked in disbelief.

"You know…like five."

I shook my head. Morgan was such a workaholic. Five really was getting out of work early for her. She was lucky to have found Patrick because most people wouldn't have been able to keep up with her.

"Yeah. That'd be good. Thanks."

She turned to leave but then glanced back over her shoulder. "You could have called, you know?"

"Yeah. Except I'm a dude."

She rolled her eyes. "Whatever, bruh."

I knew she was sincere. She would have talked it out with me or brought over a bottle of whiskey. But, for some reason, I hadn't even thought to call anyone. No one could fix what had happened. And Morgan was Sutton's sister. It didn't feel fair to dump that on her. But I guessed that was what friends were for.

After work, Morgan drove us over to the local bar Flips. It was a real townie kind of place with hardwood flooring, fluorescent lighting, and pool tables in the back. We plopped down on stools in front of a bar that had seen better days, but there was plenty of alcohol, so that was what mattered.

"Wright," the bartender, Peter, said to Morgan when she sat down. "What can I get you?"

"Stella. Make it two."

He popped the bottle caps off the tops and then passed them over to us. Morgan handed him a credit card and asked him to keep it open. For me apparently. Not her because she was driving.

"So...Sutton. Fill me in."

"You can probably imagine what happened."

"My sister is a rare breed. I never know exactly what's going to happen with her."

I shrugged and then filled her in. How we'd had our second date, and things had gotten heated, and then the next day, poof. Just like that, back to square one. Or maybe worse. Maybe I'd been moved off the board. Because, at least before, I'd had a chance, standing on the sidelines. Now, she had no interest in even being friends with me.

"Okay. Well, she probably needs time," Morgan said logically.

"I know."

"Like, a lot of time. Her husband died."

"I'm not unaware of any of this. I think it's perfectly reasonable for her to question what's happening along the way. I get where she's coming from on Jason. If she doesn't want us to be together when he's around, I can respect that, too."

"But she still broke up with you."

"Yeah, she did."

"Maybe she's really not ready."

"Maybe."

"You don't think that's it?"

"No, I believe what she says. I don't know; something she said rubs me wrong, and I can't figure it out."

"Everything she said rubs you wrong," she said, bringing the bottle to her lips.

"Maverick's parents had been there. They had Jason. Maybe they'd influenced her."

"Well, I could definitely see that. I've met them before. Good old Ray and Linda," Morgan said dryly. "They live on a farm in a rural area outside of Lubbock. They're not exactly...progressive, and they lost their son last year. I'm sure they'd spit all sorts of fear into Sutton."

I shrugged. I didn't know them, and I couldn't judge. "Even if they did, she had to already have those fears, right? They're not making her feel this way without it also coming from herself."

"True."

We lapsed into silence as I ruminated on all of that. I drank my beer and ordered a second. A good buzz might help to loosen me up, but it wasn't going to make me figure out this mystery any better.

"Maybe I should try to talk to her again."

"Nope," Morgan said. "You should give her some space. If it's just Mav's parents' fears clogging her mind, then she'll come around. If it's for real, then you're shit out of luck."

My eyes caught Morgan's, and I gave her a steadying look. "I can't give up on her. For the first time in a year, I saw her really relax and open up. I don't want to walk away from that."

"I know, but that's not always your choice."

"Do you think we were irresponsible about Jason?"

She held her hands up. "I don't have kids. I don't know what that's like."

"Theorize."

"Maybe it was too soon?" she offered. "Only Sutton can answer that."

"She was the one who invited me over."

"Second-guessing your choices is the nature of grief. Everyone grieves differently, and Sutton has been doing this almost entirely alone for a year. Being a mom is not just a part of her; it's who she is. If she feels like she's threatened Jason in any way, she's going to clam up. You have to be ready and willing to be there if she comes back out of her shell."

"I am."

Morgan nodded and tapped my hand. "Good. I thought so. Plus...I could maybe talk to her and see where her head's at."

"You don't have to do that for me." I finished the second beer, and the bartender handed me a third.

"You're my friend and my CFO. I need your head in the game. So, I'm going to talk to my sister. That's about as much as I can do."

"Thanks, Mor."

"I'm also going to get you drunk. So, bottoms up."

She raised her bottle to mine, and I clinked it against hers. She smiled, and I smiled. Then, she made me drink until I was nearly falling over, and she had to walk me into my house. I passed out cold before she even left the house. Such a great friend.

Sixteen

Sutton

"Thank y'all for watching Jason," I said, smiling down at my son, who was deeply engrossed in the television show I'd put on for him before the girls arrived. "I feel like all I've done lately is ask you to watch him."

"Well, one, that's my job," Jenny said.

"And, two, we love the little guy. I love that you're having more of a life again," Annie told me. "I don't mind."

"Me either."

"I appreciate it nonetheless." I flipped my head upside down and yanked it into a tight ponytail. Running after a two-year-old never gave me enough time to get ready. "How do I look?"

"Like you're going to pick out bachelorette party goodies," Annie said. "I'm so jealous about this. I am all about the penis."

Jenny shook her head.

"You know what I mean!"

"Oh, we do," I assured her.

"What about you?" Annie asked accusingly. "Have you gotten any of the D yet?"

I cringed and turned back to the mirror to swipe some mascara onto my sad lashes. "Nope."

I watched in the mirror as Annie shot Jenny a knowing look. *Great. Here it comes.* I had dodged a best-friend talk all week by running out the door as soon as Jenny showed up and feigning being tired as soon as I got home. Annie had been so busy at work that I might or might not have been avoiding her calls. I could fake it in a text but not when we were in person.

Where the hell is Morgan anyway? She was supposed to be here already to pick me up to take me shopping. I hadn't intended to be here a minute longer than necessary.

Really smart. Now, I was avoiding my friends and not just my in-laws.

"Something happen with David?" Annie asked.

"We're kind of on a hiatus," I admitted.

"Why?" Jenny said.

"Because I asked him to be."

"For how long?" Annie asked.

I turned to face them as I said, "Indefinitely."

"Oh, boy. What happened?" Jenny said.

"I decided I wasn't ready. I mean, besides *me*, this has got to be hard on Jason. He knows David, but this is all so new. I shouldn't have brought David here in a romantic sense until I was sure that this would last. What happens if it doesn't work out, and then I bring another guy over? It's just...irresponsible."

Jenny raised her eyebrows. "You are the last person I would ever call irresponsible."

"I wouldn't go that far," Annie said with a laugh. "You did have an oops pregnancy, but you are a hundred percent there for Jason for everything."

"It's very obvious he's your number one priority," Jenny added.

"You would never have started talking to David if you hadn't already thought through Jason's feelings. I can't think this is what you really want."

I held up my hand. "Y'all, what I want doesn't really matter. I don't want Jason to grow up, confused by who I'm dating. I don't know when and how that would affect him. I can't plan for that, except to date on the down-low. And, right now, I'm not prepared to move forward with something like that."

Annie stood and put her hands on her hips. "I get where you're coming from, but you can't hole up forever and then blame it on Jason."

"I'm not."

"You are," Jenny countered.

"Stop ganging up on me."

"Stop making us!" Annie said with a laugh. "We care about you *and* Jason. We want you to be happy."

"I am happy."

Both Annie and Jenny gave me sad faces, as if I didn't even know how miserable I really was. As if they were the only ones who saw it and I was oblivious to it.

No, I knew I was lying. I wasn't happy. I was coasting. I had Jason, and I'd thought that would be enough. But it wasn't.

Jenny touched Annie's arm, and she sat back down. "If you think you're not ready and it's better for Jason, okay."

"But you're not doing this alone. You have us," Annie told me.

"Thanks, y'all. You're really the best."

A knock on the door made all of us jump. But it was Jason who hopped up from the floor and ran to the front door. I followed Jason and cracked it open, and Morgan stood there, smiling.

"Jason!" Morgan scooped him up into her arms.

"Aunt Mor!"

"Oh, I missed you. Look at how big you are." She kissed him on both cheeks and then set him on his feet.

"Hey, Morgan," I said.

"You ready to go?"

"Yep. All set." I turned back to my friends. "A million thanks for this again. You're the best."

"Have fun! Buy me a penis or two," Annie said with a grin.

Morgan and I wore equally disgruntled looks before disappearing from the house. Her Mercedes was parked in my driveway, and we drove easily across town to the local party store.

"I can't believe I ended up being in charge of this," Morgan said in disbelief.

"Didn't you volunteer?"

"Heidi's an overlord. As the maid of honor, she doles out commands like a drill sergeant. I thought it would be easier to volunteer than to get stuck with something even more horrendous."

"I should have thought of that. I had to find the strip club."

Morgan burst into laughter. "Oh...this should be good."

"You think Heidi wanted an all-guys' strip club, right? Because there were some gentlemen's clubs that looked even more fun. But probably dicks in the face, right?"

Morgan couldn't keep it together as she parked the car. "Man, they really should have thought this through better. Imagine Emery with male strippers in her face. She's going to *kill* Heidi for doing this."

"She should expect it." I hopped out of the car, and together, we walked into the store. "It's Heidi after all. I'm more concerned for Kimber."

"This isn't the worst thing she's ever seen Emery do."

"God, I can't wait until next weekend."

"Same."

We trudged up and down the aisles until we found a giant stash of bachelorette party paraphernalia. Penis popsicles, penis straws, penis headbands, penis confetti, a blow-up doll with a giant protruding penis, a *Bride* tiara, *Team Bride* pins, a *Bride-to-Be* feather boa, and—my favorite—name tags that read *Hello, My Name Is Bitch* or *Hello, My Name Is Slut*.

"We're getting these," I said, grabbing the name tags. "I want to be the Virgin."

"You have a kid."

"So?"

Morgan rolled her eyes. "Let's get everything. I'm going to bring a whole suitcase full of dicks on the flight to Vegas. I sure hope TSA checks my bags."

We cleared out the penis aisle, and I wasn't even embarrassed about it. I thought it was going to be pretty kickass to do Emery's bachelorette party in

Vegas. All of the bridesmaids—Heidi, Kimber, Julia, Morgan, and me—were flying out for the trip, and Heidi had planned almost everything.

I hadn't gotten to have a real bachelorette party before I married Mav. I'd been knocked up, and I hadn't even been able to drink at my own reception. That part had totally sucked. Everything else had been great.

Morgan grabbed a giant lifelike penis water bottle in her hand. "Do we need this?"

I snorted and pulled my camera out. "Hold still. Let me get a good shot."

Morgan promptly pretended to deep-throat the water bottle. And I was laughing so hard that I almost fell over, which started our laughter up all again.

"Okay, okay. For real," Morgan said, trying to regain her composure. "Can I talk to you about something?"

"While you're holding that penis?"

She glanced at it and then back at me. "Yeah."

"Should I be taking you seriously?"

"I have a really mopey David at work."

My smile slipped off my face. "Oh."

"Yeah, oh. I'm not meaning to be in your business. I get that you've had a horrible year, and you've changed a lot. You're not the same person you were before Mav…you know?"

"Yeah."

"Dating again isn't going to be easy. I wouldn't expect it to. I don't know what I would do if Patrick…" Her throat closed up, and she looked like she'd be sick at the very thought.

I didn't blame her for that reaction.

I still got like that when I thought about Mav.

Except I'd thought we were invincible. Just like superheroes. But we weren't. We were regular people. One who had died and one who had died on the inside.

"I know what you're saying," I told her.

"Just talk to him, okay?"

"I can't talk to him."

Morgan pointed the penis cup at me. "I know you need your space. I'm sure having feelings for him was all new and scary again. Plus, I can totally understand your fear about Jason, but just hear David out."

"Morgan—"

"Just hear him out," she repeated. She dropped her arm. "He would never want to hurt you or Jason."

"I know," I whispered.

"If you know, then what?"

I helplessly shrugged my shoulders. "There's this fear that builds inside me when I consider dating again. When I think of what Jason will think in a year, two years, ten years. Will he resent me for bringing men into his life? Will he be as messed up as I am without one of his parents?"

"Sutton," Morgan said with a sigh. "You're not messed up because of Mom. You're messed up because Dad was a raving alcoholic, and you were raised by us. And we were just kids. It's not going to be like that for Jason because he has *you*."

"You're right," I said, sniffling and hating myself for getting teared up once again. "I just worry. And dating complicates everything."

"It does. But David is one of the good ones. I consider him a friend, and I don't make those easily. He's been here a year, and I can't shake the guy."

I laughed over a hiccup.

She pointed the penis at me again. "Just talk to him."

"Okay. I'll talk to him, but...put that penis down."

Morgan laughed and dropped the penis cup into our cart. "My work here is done."

"It might not be today...or tomorrow," I told her.

"When you're ready, Sut. Whenever you're ready."

I nodded along, but I really didn't know when that would be. Everyone made it seem like it would be so easy to pick back up where I'd left off. And I wanted it to be. But I couldn't seem to get my feet under me. I kept tripping over myself and face-planting.

I wished Maverick were here to tell me what to do. But I knew he'd never be here again. And it hardly made sense to want to talk to him about dating someone else, but I did. I missed having my best friend around. I missed the father of my child. I missed it being so easy to just breathe. To feel. To love.

Seventeen

Sutton

I didn't try to talk to David.

Part of me had wanted to call him right after Morgan dropped me back off at home. But I hadn't. I couldn't make myself do it. Not with all the fears and anxiety still pulsing through me. When we had that talk again, I wanted to be more ready. More secure. I didn't want to fall into the trap of doing this over and over again. He deserved better than that.

On Tuesday afternoon, Jason and I piled all of our stuff into the Audi and drove over to Landon's house. Before he had to leave to go back out on the professional golf tour, he was hosting a pool party for our aunt and cousins. They were supposed to return to Vancouver the next day. We'd spent some time together over the weekend, and I was sad to see them go.

But I was excited to use Landon's private pool overlooking the Wright golf course, which had had its first professional tournament in June. Also Landon's first competition he had competed in after his injury healed.

When we arrived at the party, Jason ignored everyone and rushed straight to Bethany's side, who was standing by Kimber on the first step of the pool. I shook my head. *That boy.*

After depositing our bags, I stripped out of my shorts and tank and followed my kid into the wading area of Landon's enormous pool. It was the best view in Lubbock outside of the canyons, which West Texas had like holes in Swiss cheese.

"Hey, Sutton!" Kimber said as she somehow managed to watch both Jason and Bethany play in the shallow end and keep an eye on the ever-adventurous Lilyanne in the deep end. She was superwoman.

"Hey, Kimber. How's the water?"

"Amazing. Get in."

I knotted my hair up, plopped a big, floppy hat on my head, and then entered the pool, glad that I'd applied a thick layer of sunscreen on both me and Jason before leaving the house. Kimber was right. The water was absolutely what I needed after a long day at the bakery. I'd moved on from cupcakes, and everything seemed harder than that. But still satisfying.

Jensen was at the grill with Landon coaxing him on proper technique while Aunt Helene and Julian stood nearby. Austin and Patrick were egging Lilyanne on to jump from the diving board. Bunch of jokesters. Heidi, Emery, and Julia were currently seated in a row, sunbathing. Well, Heidi mostly. Emery had her knees up and was deeply engrossed in a book. Julia had a baseball cap over her eyes and might have been asleep. My eyebrows rose considerably when I saw Annie standing awfully close to my cousin Jordan. I knew that look *all* too well.

Jenny had been standing by them but gave up and jumped into the pool next to Kimber and me. "Hey, Sut. Thank God you're here. Save me from Annie."

"That's going to be trouble, isn't it?" I asked.

"Definitely," Jenny agreed.

Jason called my attention, and Jenny and I watched him play with Bethany.

"Trouble?" Kimber asked.

"Annie and Jordan," I said, tilting my head toward them.

Her eyes skipped to where I'd been looking, and she laughed. "I know that kind of trouble. It's the good kind."

"Not with Annie," I said halfheartedly.

Who cared if Annie played her games with Jordan? He'd be gone in the morning.

"She's a bit of a hot mess," Jenny said.

"Well, more power to her at that age," Kimber said with a grin.

I moved deeper into the pool and splashed around with my son, lifting him into the air and dropping him back down in the water. He laughed and laughed and begged me to do it again. These were the days I lived for.

My arms aching, I finally yielded the game to Austin, who had moved back into the shallow end. I was shaking my arms out when I saw a figure walk into the backyard in nothing but sea-foam green swim trunks and six-pack abs. My heart went from zero to sixty in two-point-three seconds. As fast as a Bugatti.

David Calloway looked like a god. Living at the gym really worked for him. He had a runner's build, but he lifted weights enough that his abs, arms, and chest were incredibly defined. It was impossible to look away.

Even when his eyes found mine.

Even when he smiled that brilliant smile at me.

Even when I knew I should stop looking.

It had been over a week since I forced David out of my life. And two-point-three seconds after I saw him, I knew I had made a mistake.

———

The smart thing would have been to go over there and talk to him, like I'd promised Morgan. I knew that needed to happen. We had a lot to discuss. I wasn't going to apologize for how I felt, but I would apologize for how I'd treated him. I'd pushed him away out fear that had festered inside me. That wasn't fair to David. It honestly wasn't even fair to myself.

I'd do things differently this time and try to prepare myself for any other hiccups. Like total meltdowns over being a widow and having to raise my son alone.

"Do you mind keeping an eye on Jason?" I asked Kimber.

"Of course. I'll just be here."

"Thanks."

I took a deep breath and then exited the water. I snagged a towel and dried off, adjusted my hat, and then went for it. This was going to be…fun.

Morgan saw me approaching David and made a beeline for where the girls were sunbathing. Yeah, I didn't want to be here for this awkward conversation either.

David gave me a wary smile. I could tell it was forced, as if he wasn't sure if I would welcome him or assault him. Just great. This was what I'd done.

"Hey, David."

"Sutton," he said with a tilt of his head.

He glanced behind me to where my son was playing in the pool and then back to me. A pang burst in my heart.

"When Morgan invited me, I didn't really think about the fact that you probably wouldn't want me here around Jason. Should I leave?"

"No," I said quickly. My hand darted out and touched his forearm. I pulled back and tried to smile again. "No, I don't want you to leave."

"Okay. I can try to steer clear of him if that's what you want. I don't want to make you uncomfortable or anything. This is your family."

"I'm not uncomfortable."

He nodded once. His body was tense, as if he wasn't sure what to say. I'd stolen his confidence from him, and now, he was worried in my presence. I didn't like that one bit.

"David...do you think we can..."

But I was interrupted from finishing by my aunt yelling and pushing Julian into the pool. The splash drew everyone's attention. He nearly landed on top of Jenny, and she screamed as water cascaded over her hair. We all started laughing as he came up out of the water, sputtering for breath, still in a T-shirt and tennis shoes. He tugged his shoes off and tossed them out of the pool as he apologized profusely to

Jenny, who turned beet red. His mother was still laughing at him.

Then, I saw movement. Jordan drew Annie away to the house. Yeah, I wasn't stupid; I knew what was happening there.

"What were you saying?" David asked.

"I think Jordan and Annie are going to get into trouble."

David laughed. "Seems like it."

"Can't take her anywhere."

"Excuse me. Excuse me," Aunt Helene said before Julian could get out of the pool. "I'd like everyone's attention. Can you all come closer, please?"

I glanced at David and shrugged, and we moved to where my aunt was standing. Julian jumped hastily out of the pool and was speaking rapidly to his mother. But she ignored him, pushing him away.

"Not now, Julian."

"Mother," he hissed.

I'd never heard him speak that way to anyone, let alone his mom. He was the quiet type, always keen to make other people comfortable, ahead of himself. He was the baby, like I was, and we kind of had that bond. Though I had always been quick to bring a smile and tell an outrageous story. We fit in the same way as Wrights.

"I don't care what you say, Julian Wright. I am going to say my piece."

He sighed and took a step back. His face was ashen. "Fine."

"This has been such a magical week for me," Helene said, smiling at all of our family congregated around us. "It's been nearly thirty years since I left

Lubbock, and I still consider it my home. Meeting each and every one of you has made it clear that it's time to come back."

My mouth dropped open. *Oh my God! Aunt Helene is going to move to Lubbock again?*

"I've been considering this for a long time. Longer than you could possibly know. I have friends in Vancouver still, but this is my home. And I want to live my final years here."

"Final years?" Jensen asked with a tilt of his head and a furrow of his brows.

He'd asked the question we were all wondering. *What the hell did that mean?*

"You have been an excellent host, Jensen, but I'm afraid I haven't been entirely honest with you…any of you. Jordan, Julian, and I believed it would be better if I came here under the pretext of a vacation so that I could see my old home and get to know you as you see me now. Healthy, happy, vibrant even. I wanted us to become friends before you found out that I had cancer."

A pin could have dropped outside. Even the kids were silent. Even the water had ceased lapping. Only I could hear the ringing in my ears at that word. That horrible, horrible word. The one that had wrecked my family from the start. That had taken my mother and ruined my father and left me parentless.

Cancer.

No!

Not Helene, too.

Not another person I cared for.

"I've been battling it for many years. It came. It went. I fought. I won. I survived. Over and over," she said with a sigh. "And, now, it's back again, and it's spreading, so I have to fight again. And I hate to put this on all of you, but the doctors think that I won't be able to move again after we start treatments. So, I'm going to do it now. I'm going to move back, start a new treatment at the Medical Center here, and hope for the best."

Julian stepped forward then. "We didn't mean to manipulate you. That was never our intention. We just…wanted her to enjoy her time before she was the aunt with cancer."

"I don't feel manipulated," Jensen said at once and then pulled Helene in for a hug. "I'm glad you'll be here. Let me know how we can help."

Tears rimmed Helene's eyes. "Thank you."

"We'll do everything we can," Landon said, coming up for a hug, too.

Everyone pushed in tighter. Trying to get to Helene and welcome her home and wish her the best and do everything they could for her in this dark time.

And me?

I just stood there.

Frozen.

Unmoving.

Cathartic.

Because…how could this keep happening to people I cared about?

What's next? Who else is it going to happen to?

It didn't seem like an *if,* rather a when.

Eighteen

David

"Sutton," I said, cautiously placing a hand on her shoulder.

She was white as a ghost. Her mouth hung open slightly, and she looked like she might vomit or faint. I tried to draw her attention away from her aunt.

"Hey, Sutton, why don't we get you out of here?"

"Hmm?" she asked, as if going through a wind tunnel.

"I think you need a minute to regroup."

"Okay," she murmured listlessly.

I placed a hand on her back and carefully maneuvered her out of the backyard. She felt stiff and motionless as the reality about Helene sank in. She was dying. Another person Sutton loved was dying. I could already see she was drowning.

We moved through the glass double doors into the cool, air-conditioned interior of Landon's house. It was a giant open floor plan with high-vaulted, wood-beamed ceilings. Everything was contemporary rustic and looked like it cost a fortune. I was pretty sure that it was Landon who had the discerning tastes and Heidi who liked to accent things in pink.

"Take a seat."

I gestured for her to sit on a barstool, and she stared blankly forward.

"Hey, it's going to be okay. Your aunt still has a fighting chance. There's no guarantee that this is the end for her. And, in either case, none of this is your fault."

She tilted her head to look at me. I saw the years of sorrow wash over her youthful face. She was scarred from the pain of all the deaths in life. Internal emotional scarring that nothing could ever erase or heal.

"Sutton, you have a wonderful life. A son who loves you with all his big heart. Four siblings who think the world of you. Two best friends and a great job. You have…me," I offered carefully. "You have so much. Your entire life isn't just…this."

"I know," she said.

Then, she stood on her tiptoes and kissed me.

Her lips were soft and tender and inviting. These were the lips I'd been dreaming about long before she kissed me. Yet…this was wrong.

She was only doing this out of grief for what she had heard. Her sadness and her mourning and her pain had led her to this moment. I would never take advantage of her. I couldn't do it. I wanted more from her than that, and it wouldn't be right to take it in a moment of weakness.

With difficulty, I placed my hands on her shoulders and pushed her away. "Sutton…no."

"No?" she asked in confusion.

"Why don't we go for a walk and get you some fresh air?"

"But, wait...I thought this was what you wanted?"

"It is. It was," I corrected. "But not like this. Not when you're doing it in reaction to something else."

She nodded, and I could see shame cross her face. "I'm sorry."

"Let's just walk."

"I am sorry," she repeated.

"I know."

We moved out of the house and away from the rest of the party. Neither of us looked back to see what was happening. We moved farther across the backyard and onto the golf course that Landon's house had been built on. A gravel trail wound around the course, large enough for a golf cart, and we walked along it, away from the house and all its responsibilities.

"I can't go through another death," Sutton finally said.

"You don't know that she's going to die."

"With my luck..."

"That's not true. It's the grief talking. You have no bearing on whether or not your aunt beats her cancer. The best you can do is get to know her while she's here. She clearly came here for a reason, and she loves you all enough to tell the truth."

"Yeah, the truth. What a burden." She shook her head and sighed. "I don't mean to sound this down. I am happy that she's here. I like her a lot and wish that we had known her our whole lives. But, fuck, it sucks."

137

"It does. It really does. Death like that…even just the thought of death, it fucks with you. It shreds you from the inside out. Time might numb it, but it never really heals."

Sutton's eyes crept over to mine. "Exactly. How do you always know the right thing to say?"

I blushed and turned my face away. I felt a pang in my chest. I should tell her everything. Reveal the past I kept so close to me. That no one knew, and I never wanted anyone to know. But this was real, and she deserved my truth. Except…everything was still so precarious.

"David?" she asked quietly.

"My best friend committed suicide."

It took me a second before I realized that Sutton had stopped entirely at my words. She was standing a few feet behind me.

I turned around to look at her. "What?"

"Your best friend committed suicide? You never told me that."

"You never asked."

"This whole year, you were here for me through what happened with Maverick. You never pushed me. You never tried to make me feel guilty about the pain. You never tried to make me get over it. You never even had a misstep where you just said something that I'd heard a million times before and was so over…like that stupid fucking phrase, *Everything happens for a reason.* You never said any of that."

"No, I didn't."

"Why did you never tell me?"

"I didn't want your pain to be about me."

All the tension left her body. "Really?"

"Everyone grieves differently. Everyone's pain is different. I could be here for you, but I couldn't console you. Because no one could console me when Holli took her own life. They could be there for me, but nothing could change what happened. No one else's stories made me feel better."

"Exactly," Sutton said. She reached out and tenderly, deliberately touched my arm. "Tell me what happened."

My throat closed up at the thought of talking about Holli. I'd told the story before. It had been nearly fifteen years before, and still, it choked me up. "It was a week before school got out our sophomore year of high school. Nothing was wrong. Holli had always been…dark. Like she saw the world as bleak. But I'd known her my entire life. When it looked bad, she always got help. Then, suddenly, it was as if everything was finally better. She was really doing well in school, she had all these plans for summer break, and she'd finally gotten her first boyfriend. Then, I got a call from Holli in class. She'd skipped that day, but it wasn't out of the norm. I didn't answer. An hour later, her mom found her with a bullet between her forehead and blood down her white walls."

Sutton gasped and threw her hand to her mouth. "Oh my God. That's awful."

"It was. Holli was really more like my only friend. She was smart and funny and quirky. She liked to play lacrosse and video games. She doodled on all of her notebooks. She could wear high fashion in one breath and ratty sweats the next and still look effortless. She had everything going for her, and she's still gone. And there's nothing I could have done to stop it…except answer that phone call."

"You don't know that."

"And, fifteen years later, it still haunts me."

Sutton nodded at me, understanding blooming in her eyes. It was like we understood each other completely for the first time. Something passed between us then that I'd never felt in my life. I'd felt connected to Sutton from the start. But having it out in the open, what had happened with Holli, seemed to change everything in a way I'd never thought possible. I'd wanted to keep it to myself so as not to burden her or try to redirect the conversation about her grief. But it was clear that telling her what had happened and why I was so attuned to what she was going through had opened her eyes.

"I don't remember the last thing Maverick said to me," she confessed.

"Does it kill you?"

"Yes. I try to remember constantly, but it's just not there."

"Holli didn't even leave a note."

Sutton sighed. "That's horrible. I can't imagine how that must have felt."

"I think you can."

"Different," she conceded. "Thank you for telling me about her. She must have been very special to you."

"She was. I would have liked to see the person that she grew into."

"I know what you mean."

We stood in silence. No longer walking down the golf course path. Just standing in the shade of a tree and looking at each other. We'd come to a mutual understanding, and I liked that we could stand together without it being awkward. With the weight of our pasts not weighing us down, but lifting us up.

"Can we start over?" Sutton finally asked.

"I think I'd like that."

"I think I let my fears dictate my life. I don't want that. I still have fears, but I want to live. I shouldn't have let that hinder me in such a way, and I definitely shouldn't have lashed out at you."

"It's okay. I knew where you were coming from," I assured her.

"Thank you for understanding, but it's not fair for you to have to deal with that."

"I'm not dealing with it. It's part of who you are. You can't change how his death affected you."

"I know," she said softly. Then, she stepped forward, very close to me. "But I can change how I let it affect other people. I don't think that it's too soon for me to date. I think I'm ready."

"You're sure?"

She nodded. "I know you're not a danger to Jason. I think maybe…we should keep our romantic relationship to a minimum to begin with and see how it goes."

"That sounds reasonable to me. I would like to be his friend though, if that's all right."

"Oh, yes," she said with a broad smile. "He can always use another friend."

"You know what?" I said, moving my hand to her waist and tugging her a little closer.

"What?"

"I think I'll take that kiss now."

She giggled. "Oh, yeah? Think you deserve that kiss?"

"Come here," I growled.

I nipped her bottom lip and then melded our mouths together.

I had come to this party, thinking that the worst that could happen was an uncomfortable conversation or maybe getting kicked out. I'd never thought for a second that Sutton and I would somehow get on the exact same page. And, now, here we were. My butterfly was spreading her wings.

Nineteen

David

I stepped into Death by Chocolate at a quarter past noon. The place was packed with students who were already trickling back in before the start of the semester. I already missed the summer quiet that I'd found to be my favorite time in Lubbock. College towns had their ebbs and flows.

Sutton was scurrying back and forth behind the counter, filling orders and handing them to the thin Latina girl, Tessa, running the register. Sutton glanced up at me when I approached, and a toothy grin split her face.

"You're late," she said.

"You're busy."

"Exceptionally so."

"Should we cancel?" I asked. Though it was the last thing I wanted to do.

"No way. Let me finish these orders, and I'll be out for the day."

I nodded at her and took a table near a pair of hipsters who looked out of place in the pastel interior. Kimber found my table and passed me a piece of her famous chocolate cake.

"You're stealing my star employee!" she accused.

I laughed. "I guess I am."

"Girl needs a life, so I don't begrudge you."

"I'll come work a shift to make up for it."

She rolled her eyes. "Oh dear Lord, that would just be great for the kitchen."

Sutton appeared and then flushed, holding a box of goodies. "I'm ready. Sorry about that."

"Have fun, Sutton. See you tomorrow."

"Bye, Kimber," Sutton and I said together.

"Shall we?" I asked, taking the box from her.

I tried to get a sneak peek, but she smacked my hand.

"Not yet!"

"All right, all right. Let's go, so I can eat these."

She followed me out to the Ferrari. I was excited for this lunch I had planned. It meant I got time alone with Sutton before she left for Emery's bachelorette party, and it was during the time that Jenny already had Jason. So, as long as I got her back by five thirty, we were golden.

"Are you going to tell me where we're going?"

"That would take all the fun out of it."

She wrinkled her nose at me but didn't ask again. It was only about ten minutes later before she clearly realized where we were going. It wasn't the best-laid surprise since she'd lived here a lot longer than me. But, with the time permitting, it was the best I could do.

"Ransom Canyon?" she guessed. "Did you talk to Jensen?"

"Yep." I dangled a key in front of her, and she shook her head.

"You wrangled the cabin key from him? Amazing."

Jensen had a lake house in the canyon that all the Wrights used. They went there most holidays to hang out, go boating or tubing, and get drunk in a safe place with lots of bedrooms. Even though I'd been there a couple of times myself, I hadn't thought that Jensen would let me take Sutton there alone.

Ransom Canyon was about twenty minutes outside of downtown Lubbock, and it looked like a world of its own with giant mansion-like cabins along the water with docks and boats and Jet Skis. The property became more manageable, the higher up the canyon rim. And it was absolutely gorgeous.

Riding down the canyon walls in a Ferrari was not so great though. It was the first time I really thought that I should give in and get a truck. But a truck really wasn't me.

We parked out front, and I popped open the front trunk. It didn't hold all that much to begin with, but I'd managed to fit a picnic basket in there. Sutton opened the cabin door ahead of me as I carried the basket. She grinned at me like a fool.

"This is a fun," she told me.

"And you haven't even seen inside the basket."

She tried to open the basket a pinch, but I quickly put my hand over it.

"No cheating."

"Ugh! Fine. I'm horrible at surprises. I'll have you know, I used to open gifts at parties while people weren't looking."

"Color me shocked," I said sarcastically.

"I bet you were a good little boy and waited until you were allowed," she teased.

"I waited for you."

Her eyes were bright as she leaned over the kitchen counter. "Is that so?"

"Of course. You were worth waiting for."

She tapped my nose with her finger and winked. "Well, no more waiting now."

"Thank God."

"I'm going to go change into a suit. Thank God, I have one at the cabin."

"Yeah, Jensen mentioned that."

She stuck her tongue out at me. "Then we can eat because I'm starving, and I want to know what's in that basket!"

She skipped away to a bedroom while I changed into my swim trunks in the bathroom. I gathered towels and sunscreen from a closet, stuffed them in a bag, and was ready to go when Sutton appeared in the doorway.

She wasn't wearing the cute pale yellow suit she'd worn to Landon's pool party earlier this week. Now, she was in a black barely there bikini with lace-up bottoms and a strapless bra-esque top. It looked really fucking hot on her, and all thoughts of lunch disappeared from my mind.

"What?" she asked as if she didn't know.

"You look amazing."

She tugged on the string of her bikini. "I haven't worn this thing since college. It doesn't look ridiculous?"

"Ridiculous?" I scoffed. "No, not at all."

"You don't look so bad yourself," she said with a playful wink.

I laughed and then moved to where she was standing. I wrapped an arm around her bare waist and pulled her in for a kiss. Her smile was infectious. I could have stayed there all day if it wasn't for her stomach grumbling.

"Food it is," I said instead.

I took her hand, and we carried everything down to the dock. After laying out the blanket, we set the picnic basket down and took our seats. Sutton carefully applied a layer of sunscreen to her body while I opened the basket.

My first item made her eyes round with excitement. "Sangria!"

"La Sirena sangria."

"What?" she gasped. "How did you get that?"

"Morgan is obsessed with that place. I had her call in a favor because I know you love it."

"This doesn't seem like a fly-by-the-seat-of-your-pants kind of date."

"Well...it's not. I might or might not have already been planning this when we had our falling-out."

"Aww, that's so sweet."

"I'm glad that you gave us a second chance so that I hadn't called in all these favors for nothing."

She laughed. "You're cute. Now, food!"

I'd brought a cheese plate and sandwiches along with strawberries, raspberries, and peaches. We laughed and chatted while we finished off our lunch.

It was so nice and peaceful. The lake was quiet on a Thursday afternoon, even with kids out of school. It felt as if she and I were the only two people in this silent canyon in West Texas. And I liked it that way.

"Dessert now or later?" Sutton asked.

My eyes swept her body, and I knew exactly what I wanted for dessert. My head was a little fuzzy from the sangria, and my mouth didn't catch up with my mind. "Now."

And the way I'd said it made her blush and nearly trip over herself. "You don't even know what's for dessert."

"I could guess."

My guess was probably not Kimber's famous chocolate cake.

Sutton giggled. I didn't even know how we'd finished all of that sangria, but it was making her giggle, and, God, I loved that giggle. I loved every time she laughed. Genuine laughs were so rare from her that it was like a delicacy that needed to be savored.

"I think your mind is in the gutter."

"Me?" I gasped, coming to my feet. "Never."

"Uh-huh. I have three older brothers. I know what you mean by *dessert*."

I helped her to her feet and took a step forward, moving into her space. She didn't back away or back down. Her smile only grew.

"I'm merely curious about what you brought me for dessert. You put all the time and effort into your...treats. It's only fair that I taste-test them."

She chewed on her bottom lip, clearly reading my double meaning in all of that. And then she burst out laughing.

"I will never look at lemon bars the same again," she accused. Then, she couldn't seem to hold any of it in, and she laughed so hard, so unabashedly that she snorted. She covered her mouth in horror and tried to stop herself from laughing anymore, which did absolutely nothing, and she snorted again.

Fuck me, she was even gorgeous when she snorted.

"I think I'd like that lemon bar now," I said with my own laugh because it was impossible not to laugh when she was giggling like this.

"You'll have to get there first."

Then, she turned around and raced for the cabin. I watched her lean legs race down the dock. She glanced over her shoulder once to see if I was following her, and I took off. I could easily catch her. I ran miles and miles every morning, but this wasn't that kind of chase.

This was her laughing uninhibitedly as she stumbled up the slope back to the cabin. This was her hair whipping in the wind, nearly yanking it out of its ponytail. This was the look of sheer joy as she saw how near I was.

She dashed into the house, and I heard a click just as I reached for the handle. Locked. *Damn it!*

I watched through the glass as she went to the kitchen, returned with the box of desserts, and removed the lemon bar from the box. She took a giant bite out of the tart. A triumphant smile split her face.

"Oh, you're going to get it," I told her with a shake of my head.

She put her hand to her ear, as if to say, *What? I can't hear you.*

Then, she flipped the lock, and I barreled in after her. She shrieked and dashed toward the kitchen with the box in hand. I caught her round the middle and swung her around to face me. She held the box over her head, but she was so much shorter than me that it wasn't over *my* head.

She was panting from exertion and giddiness and anticipation. Her smile was electric and magnetic. She was as warm as a Texas summer and twice as vibrant. When I dropped my lips down on hers, she tasted like lemons. And nothing had ever been so sweet.

Twenty

Sutton

"Did you make this tart?" David asked against my lips.

I nodded breathlessly and slowly brought the box down between us. "For you. Want to try?"

He nodded.

I picked the lemon bar back out of the box, dropped the box onto the counter, and then held the treat before him. He arched an eyebrow at me and then opened his mouth. I watched him take a small bite out of the lemon tart. When he closed his eyes and groaned at the taste of it, it set me on fire.

"Dear God, this is heaven."

"Uh-huh. I think they're my signature."

He took the tart from me and dropped it back down into the box. My heart was in my throat when he tugged me closer again and started kissing his way up my neck.

"I think I'll have you for dessert instead."

"Is that so?" I asked breathily.

"Mmhmm."

My heart was hammering away in my chest, and my body was giving off mixed signals. Yes, I wanted this. No, I wasn't ready. Yes…yes, I was.

I wanted this moment with David.

I wanted and needed to be okay with this.

I'd chosen him.

He was choosing me.

David nibbled on my earlobe, dragging it between his teeth. I sighed and leaned into him. He took that as an invitation and swirled me around so that I was against the kitchen island. He had me pinned with his hips, and it was pretty obvious where his thoughts were.

I was just standing there, enjoying the attention, but I was an eager participant. Suddenly, I remembered what I was supposed to be doing with my body…my hands. I ran them down his solid chest, letting my nails trail across every ripped ab until I hit the V at his waist. He sucked in a deep breath at my advances, and it only emboldened me further.

After a moment of hesitation, I slipped a finger under the hem of his board shorts. He pressed harder against me. My pulse quickened as I felt his length through our thin clothing. He was…big. Fuck, I could tell that, and I hadn't even touched him or seen him or fucking anything. And, instead of feeling fear or pain or uncertainty, I felt only desire.

My body was hot. It was a primal need that my fingers and toys at home couldn't come close to sating. It had been a long, *long* year alone. I was too young to be alone. And I knew then that I didn't want to continue like this. I wanted David. Physically, emotionally, mentally. I wanted every bit that he was willing to give to me, and I wanted it all right now.

He cupped my jaw in both of his hands and tilted my face up to look into his golden eyes. "You are the most beautiful thing I have ever laid eyes on."

I blushed, and he left no room for a response before he thoroughly kissed me again. My hand slipped down the front of his shorts, and a moan escaped us both as I grasped his cock in my hand.

"I want you," he pleaded.

"Yes," I gasped.

"Now."

"Yes."

He tugged on the strings of my bikini, letting all the tiny pieces collapse onto the floor, forgotten. My hands were trembling slightly as I hooked my fingers into his shorts and let them meet the same fate.

I took a steadying breath. Just one. That was all I needed.

David ran his hands down my body, exploring every inch of my exposed skin. Then, he wrapped his hands around the backs of my thighs and hoisted me onto the counter. He spread my legs wider before him, and then with a devious grin, he laid me back flat.

He hooked my knee over his shoulder before dragging his tongue up the inside of my left leg. I gasped and squirmed at the sensation but had nothing further to say, except moan when he moved his tongue to my clit. Or when his fingers moved inside my pussy. Or when he pushed my leg even further open.

I ached from my core all the way to the tips of my fingers and toes. This was torture. Sweet, blissful torture. Even better than the first time on the couch. This place had none of the memories my house did. It had no consequences. It had perfect freedom. And I was riding that freedom straight to climax.

My body bucked against him as he held me down against the kitchen counter. I was trying to escape the lavish attention as my core exploded. I arched off the counter and cried out in ecstasy at the pleasure that wrecked my body.

"More," I pleaded.

I shuddered on the countertop and then sat up to reach for his cock. He groaned as I toyed with him.

"I want to suck you off," I told him, looking him dead in the eyes.

His cock jerked in my hand.

"What? No blush?" he joked.

"Not in the slightest."

"Fuck." He gripped my thigh hard and then brought his hand up to stroke my bottom lip. My body warmed up all over again at that one touch. "I want that, but I want to fuck you."

"Just a taste?" I asked.

He pressed forward until the tip of his cock moved into me. I shuddered and nearly gave in to that feeling. Wanting nothing more than for him to take me just like that. But that was what I would have done before. That was what had gotten me into my first mess. I wanted this to be different. I was different. David was different. I had control…some semblance of it.

"Condom," I forced out between my teeth.

He nodded and pulled one out of his shorts. Thank fuck he had one. Stopping would have been…difficult, to say the least.

He rolled the condom onto his length, stole another deep kiss, and then thrust deep inside me. I cried out around his lips. My walls pulsed around his cock, and my body trembled with relief and exertion.

Oh God, I wanted this. I wanted all of this.

David wrapped a steadying arm around my back and then dragged his way out of me. Then, with his eyes set on mine, he eased back in. Slow and steady and reassuring. Watching every movement to make sure that I was okay. To see that I wasn't going to break down and freak out and cry. Because that was the person I had been. That was the person who had never been able to separate what had been from what was now. To see that I could mourn that life and still enjoy this one. But I was not going to cry. I was not going to mourn. I was going to enjoy every single minute of this.

"I'm okay," I assured him.

"Are you sure?"

"I'm not going to be if you keep going that slow."

He grinned and then slammed back into me until he was seated to the hilt. I tilted my head back, and my mouth made an O as he did it again and again. He kissed me one more time and then leaned me back on the counter. Gripping my hips in his hands, he drove forward into me. Our bodies slapped together. I knew I would be sore later, but I could hardly care. It felt too fucking good.

"Sutton…I'm close," he warned me.

"Come with me," I pleaded.

Then, he buried himself in me one more time, and we both came together. My body shook from head to toe. My orgasm was so intense, I was certain I saw stars on the ceiling. He was gasping for air as he lay forward across my naked body. He kissed a soft trail across my stomach.

I stretched my arms overhead. "Remind me never to bake in this kitchen."

David chuckled once and then burst into full-on laughter. "You're perfect. You know that?"

I ran my fingers through his hair and sighed in satisfaction. "We should clean up. Then, I could use a nap. Do you know how much sleep you get with a two-year-old?"

"Not enough?"

"Not enough."

I disappeared into the bathroom and quickly cleaned up. Before I left, I looked at myself in the mirror. I looked different. Skinnier for sure. Though the bakery was helping me put those pounds back on—thankfully. But also…happier. Like I wasn't a ghost living in this body. I seemed strong again. Like this month with David had awoken me once more. I didn't feel like I was about to fall to pieces because I'd just had sex with another man. It felt good and right.

I stumbled into the first-floor guest bedroom and found David already under the covers. I crawled into bed after him.

"How are you feeling?" he asked, brushing my hair out of my face.

"Like I'm ready for round two."

He laughed and nipped at my lip. "No, really. I know that must have been hard for you. New."

"It's new. But it's not hard for me. Not right now. I know I might freak out about it later, but right now, I feel like it was the right thing to do. I wanted to be with you. I *want* to be with you, David."

"Good. I'm glad to hear that. I want to be with you, too." He brought my hand to his lips and started to kiss every single digit. "But I'm always going to put your well-being above my own. I want to do right by you."

"It was right," I assured him and then gestured to myself. "Wright even."

"Ha-ha."

"Of course, I'm conflicted because this is like a new first. You popped my cherry," I joked. "But I'm glad it was you. You made it perfect. I like that this new beginning is our new beginning. And I'm ready for that."

"Good," he said, kissing me again.

"Do you think there's another condom in this house?" I asked.

He arched an eyebrow. "I'll scour the place if you will."

"We still have a couple of hours. How much sleep do I really need?"

"Oh, I like this new beginning."

I laughed, and then we both went in search.

I was the victorious one who found three condoms in an upstairs bedroom. He was the victorious one when he got to use all three.

Twenty-One

Sutton

"Sutton, stop making that face," Morgan said the next day as I lounged in the private jet.

"What face?"

"That I'm-so-gloriously-happy face. The young love and happy times and angels singing."

I tried to frown, failing miserably as the corners of my lips turned up again. "I can't help it."

Morgan rolled her eyes. "It's so disgusting."

"What is?" Heidi asked, bouncing from foot to foot as her blonde ponytail flounced behind her.

"All the love in the air."

Heidi grinned broadly. "I think it's great! Everyone is so happy. You're happy, Mor!"

"Ugh! Where are Emery and Julia? They'll be cynical with me."

"Emery is going to be married in a couple of weeks. I don't think she's cynical about this bachelorette party," I reminded her.

"I didn't even get all the dicks I brought checked by TSA because we're taking the private jet."

"Are you complaining that we're flying private?" Emery asked as she stepped onto the airplane.

"No," Morgan said. "But it would have been epic."

"Jensen was reluctant to give us the plane since he's seeing Colton this weekend in New York, but I talked him into it."

"And how much talking was done?" Julia asked with an arched eyebrow.

Emery smirked. "You're the devil."

Julia held her hands up and then promptly plopped into a seat next to me. "I'm just saying, I know how those Wright boys are handled."

"Ew," I said at the same time Morgan said, "Gross."

Then, we looked at each other and laughed.

Kimber was the last on the plane. She glanced around in awe and shook her head. "What a way to travel."

With everyone on board, it was a quick two-hour flight to Vegas where we went through several bottles of champagne. Tipsy and giggly, we hopped into an awaiting limo and were whisked to the Bellagio where Heidi had booked us the penthouse suite. My eyes were large as saucers as I took in the massive room with four bedrooms, six bathrooms, a parlor, Jacuzzi, private sauna, pool table, and a wraparound balcony overlooking the fountains and Strip beyond.

We spent the first day at the spa with massages, facials, manicures, pedicures, and full hair and makeup, and then the real fun began.

I followed Morgan into the bedroom I was sharing with her and opened up the giant suitcase she'd stuffed full of penis paraphernalia. She started handing penises to everyone with delight, and I grabbed the package of name tags.

"Okay, I already claimed the Virgin," I said, slapping the tag onto my black minidress. We were all wearing different black dresses and heels, and Emery was in white, which was hilarious, considering she wasn't wearing white on her wedding day. "That makes you the Bride-to-Be."

I pasted the name tag to Emery's chest and glanced down at the rest. "Heidi, you're the Slut."

Heidi shrugged and took the name tag from me. "I'll take it."

"Kimber, I think you're the Drunk."

"Me?" Kimber asked. "I'm the responsible one with two kids."

"And I'm wearing the Virgin tag."

She laughed. "Okay. Drunk it is."

"Julia…"

"Bitch," she offered.

"I was going to go with Tease."

Emery giggled and grabbed the Bitch sticker. "Nope. Bitch it is."

"I love you," Julia said.

"And that leaves Morgan." I stared down at the remaining name tags.

Morgan groaned. "Hit me with your best shot."

"Hot Mess."

"Yes, the CEO is the hot mess."

"You kind of are when you get wasted though," Heidi said.

"Yeah, remember that time at First Friday?" Emery asked.

Morgan's cheeks heated. "I try not to think about that night. Thank you very much." She snatched the Hot Mess tag and slapped it onto herself. "Fine. I accept this, but only if I get a picture of everyone holding a dick."

The girls laughed and scrambled together as we all held out the random penises, and Morgan took a selfie.

"That picture does not go online," Emery said. "If my high school students saw that, I'd never hear the end of it."

Morgan held up her hands. "What happens in Vegas stays in Vegas."

"It'd better."

"Morgan will only use it to blackmail you later," I told Emery reassuringly. She groaned. "Come on. Let's head out to my part of the party."

Catcalls and cheers followed us as we traipsed through the Bellagio in our bachelorette attire. Our party was offered two rounds of shots just as we paraded through the casino, and by the time we reached our awaiting limo, I was buzzed. Maybe a bit beyond buzzed. Between the champagne on the plane and at the spa, then drinks in the room, and shots on the casino floor, I'd already had more to drink than I'd had all summer. And we still had the strip club to go.

"How fucked up am I going to get?" I whisper-yelled into Morgan's ear.

She laughed. "You're already fucked up, little sis. And, man, this is going to be fun. I don't think I've ever seen you cut loose like this."

"Just every weekend in high school and college. You must have missed it."

"Oh," Morgan said with a frown. "How did I miss that?"

"Life," I offered with a shrug.

"Well, I won't miss it this time. It's long overdue. You were always the baby. Now, we can get wasted together."

I giggled and leaned into her. "This is the best."

Our limo dropped us off out front of the place I'd chosen. It had been interesting, to say the least, to do the research for this. Most of the big male strip shows in Las Vegas had several hundred women inside, and the guys danced for you. I'd found a place that was much more exclusive where the male dancers came to dance for you at your table, onstage, and in private rooms. I knew Emery would probably be so embarrassed, but I'd been to one of these before in college, and it outweighed the shows any day of the week.

We were seated in a VIP booth with bottle service, and as soon as we had drinks in front of us, guys flocked to our table. A waitress popped open a bottle of Patrón, and the table—dancers and all—did shot after shot.

I was spinning in a circle—or maybe that was just my head. Everything was lights and sounds and dancing. I was laughing and falling into people in my high heels. Nearly naked men in banana hammocks were grinding up on everyone, and I couldn't stop giggling.

"Private dance!" I cried, tossing money at the cutest dancer.

He tried to grab my hand to take me back to a room, but I shook my head.

I pointed at my name tag. "I'm a Vir-gin. Virrrr-gin."

He laughed. "Not for long, honey."

"Dance is for the bride." I stumbled a step forward, tried to clear the blurriness from my eyes, and pointed at Emery. "Her!"

"No, no, no, no, no," Emery said. She waved her hands in front of her. "No private dances for me."

"I've already...p-paid!"

"You take the dance then."

"I'm a Vir-gin, Em. Vir-gin."

Someone snorted behind me. And I whipped around fast, nearly falling over. I was laughing my ass off, too, because, nothing had ever been so funny.

A hand landed on my waist to try to help me up. I turned to the cute dancer I had bought a lap dance from for Emery and leaned in close. "Want to know a secret?"

He arched his perfectly manicured eyebrows. "What's that, love?"

"I'm not a Vir-gin," I whispered. Or I thought I'd whispered.

He laughed. "I'm shocked."

"I've had *a lot* of sex."

"Congratulations. Me, too."

"I had sex yesterday!"

"Nice!"

The guy high-fived me. I missed.

"Oh my God, try again. I'm so white."

He was really laughing at me now. "You're adorable. We should do a shot to celebrate you having sex yesterday."

"Wait, what?" Morgan said. "You had sex yesterday?"

"I had sex yesterday!" I cheered.

"Oh my God! Oh my God, oh my God, oh my God!" Morgan grabbed my hands and jumped around in a circle. I teetered around with her, feeling like I was going to topple over at any moment. "You got laid!"

"I got laid!" I cried.

Then, suddenly, all the girls were in on it, cheering me on for having had sex yesterday. I felt no judgment. Or fear or ache about it. I felt like I was on top of the world. It didn't matter that I'd imbibed nearly enough alcohol to kill me. This was right. This was perfect.

I was jumping around and deliriously happy with my girls.

Even the strippers were crying out with us, "She got laid!"

This was a feeling I'd never forget but probably a night I'd never remember.

Twenty-Two

Sutton

My head felt like it had been kicked, been run over, and then had a ton of bricks dropped on it. Opening my eyes made the entire room spin.

"Up and at 'em, sunshine," Morgan said, slicing the curtains open.

I groaned and turned away from the blinding light. "Why did I drink that much?"

"Because you're young, and that's what you're supposed to do."

"Shh," I grumbled. "Lower the volume."

"Oh no. Last night, I got way more details than I'd ever thought I'd need to know about David. You do realize, I have to work with him still. Like, next door. Every day. You could have left some details out."

My eyes flew open, and I shot up in bed. "I did, *what*?"

I then immediately regretted that decision as my hangover carved through my brain and incinerated me from the inside out.

"Yeah. Yep. Uh-huh," Morgan muttered.

I covered my face with my hands. "Oh God. Well…shit."

"That's about where I'm at, too."

"You cannot repeat any of that to him."

"Yeah, as if I'm going to bring up the exact measurements of his dick in regular conversation," Morgan said with a dramatic eye roll. "I'm a CEO. I know when discretion is necessary."

"I am so sorry that conversation happened. And, wow, I don't remember any of it."

"You should be so glad you don't remember the rest. Now, get up. We're getting brunch."

"Ugh, what time is it?"

"It's already one, and I'm starving."

I nodded and then slowly rolled off the bed. After I brushed my teeth and took a quick shower, I started to feel a little better. A semblance of myself at least. I still couldn't believe that I'd told anyone that David and I had slept together, let alone the depth and breadth of information I'd apparently shared.

Those drinking business meetings really must have helped her. I'd tried to stay away from alcohol since Maverick's passing. I'd worried I'd end up like our father, and that had done enough not to let me wallow in a bottle. Even though, for a long time, I'd thought it'd be easier.

I finished blowing out my hair and moved into the foyer. "We ready?"

"We're still waiting on Heidi," Emery said with a yawn. "She's been throwing up all morning."

"God, is she that hungover?"

Emery shrugged her shoulder. "I told her some food would help, but she keeps throwing up. I swear, it's not like her either."

"Let me check on her one more time," Julia said.

A few minutes later, a pale Heidi appeared next to Julia. She looked like a wreck. I felt like shit, but at least I hadn't thrown up. I hated throwing up. I fought it with every fiber of my being.

Heidi stuck her thumb up. "Let's do this."

Emery gave her a side-eye and then nodded.

We were a motley crew compared to how we'd looked last night, glamorous and done up. We had to half-drag our party downstairs and to the brunch place by the pool. There was a line, but since we were VIPs, they held a table at the back for our party. As soon as we sat, Heidi was up and rushing to the restroom.

"Geez," Morgan said. "I didn't think she had that much more than me. I feel fine."

"I feel like shit," I grumbled.

"You had way more to drink though," Kimber pointed out.

"Oh," I whispered. Then, a thought struck me. "Oh!"

"What?"

"Oh my God, is she pregnant?" I gasped.

Kimber's jaw dropped. "Oh, she's so pregnant."

"What?" Emery stammered. "No way!"

Morgan shook her head and blinked rapidly.

Julia opened her mouth and then closed it. "I have no idea."

"Having had a kid...I'd say she's definitely preggers. I mean, you said she didn't have as much to drink as I did. I feel like shit. You feel fine. She doesn't normally throw up. She has morning sickness."

Kimber nodded emphatically. "I can't believe I didn't see it at once."

Emery's eyes were wide. "She's going to kill me."

"Definitely," Julia agreed.

"It's not like you got her pregnant," I said with a laugh.

"Oh no, but I got her wasted."

Just then, a rather pallid Heidi reappeared at the table. "Hey, y'all. Sorry. I cannot kick this hangover."

The table fell silent. We all glanced back and forth around at each other. No one wanted to make eye contact with Heidi.

"What? What happened? Is everything okay?" Heidi gasped. She clutched her stomach and bit her lip.

"Heidi," I said calmly, "I think you're pregnant."

I hadn't thought it possible, but Heidi paled even further.

"What?" she whispered.

Kimber reached out and clutched Heidi's hand. "When was your last period? Could this be morning sickness rather than a hangover?"

"Oh no," Heidi muttered. "Oh no! I cannot be pregnant right now! No, it was supposed to take longer than this."

"What was?" Emery asked.

"We…we started trying, but I was told it could take a couple of months once I got off birth control for everything to even out. I didn't think…well…*this*."

"You started trying," Emery gasped, jumping to her feet. "Oh my God, Heidi!"

"But I'm not pregnant! I got trashed last night. I could have killed this little fetus thing inside me with fetal alcohol poisoning. Oh my God, we all got so drunk last night."

We all laughed at her melodrama.

"You'll be fine," Kimber assured her. "You're not the first woman to get drunk in the first trimester without knowing about it."

"I'm going to kill you," Heidi said, pointing her finger in Emery's face.

We all busted out laughing as Emery's prediction came true.

"Don't laugh. It's her fault I got that drunk last night. And Landon's fault if this is fucking true." She covered her mouth, groaned, and dashed to the restroom again.

We finished off a quick brunch and then headed to the closest convenience store we could find. We bought three packets of pregnancy tests and forced Heidi into the penthouse bathroom. After a half-dozen tests that were all positive, Heidi burst into tears, and we were all dancing around her in excitement.

"Landon is going to be so happy!" I told her consolingly.

"I'm happy," she said through the tears, "and terrified."

"It's all right. That's normal. Kimber and I have been through this. You'll do great."

"Even better," Kimber said, patting her hand.

"We're going to have to throw you a party!" Emery told her. "Before the wedding."

"Not before the wedding," Heidi said. "I'm not taking the limelight."

"No way! You're pregnant; we have to celebrate. We'll have a shower later when you're showing. And, oh my God, we're going to have to do pregnancy pictures."

"Since when do you care about babies?"

"Since my best friend is fucking pregnant, you whore!" Emery said, laughing.

"Hey, she likes my kids," Kimber said.

"I do," Emery admitted. She turned back to Heidi. "Why don't we head back early tomorrow so that you can tell Landon?"

"What? No! We can't end this early!"

"As if you're up for another night of partying. We had a great time last night, but maybe we can just relax tonight."

"If by relax, you mean gambling, then fine," Heidi said.

Her demeanor had shifted, and I could already tell that she was glowing with the news. Maybe it wasn't the best time for her to be pregnant, but now that she had come to terms with it, she seemed ecstatic.

That was how I'd been, too. Shocked by the possibility of being pregnant out of wedlock to a guy I'd met in college, who I had no idea I'd want to marry. Then, immediately had a shotgun wedding and the most beautiful baby boy. She was going to love it. I knew that for certain.

———

As Emery wished, we had a quiet night of gambling. Then, we ended up watching rom-coms on the giant flat screen while eating loads of ice cream and giggling like schoolgirls. It had to be one of the most fun nights of my life.

We took the private jet back early the next morning, groggy and puffy-eyed. We dragged ourselves off the jet, only to find Jensen waiting for us on the runway.

Emery rushed to him, and without a care for the rest of us, she wrapped her legs around his waist and thoroughly kissed him. Morgan and I exchanged a look of disgust and a good-natured giggle.

"You're back early," Jensen said with an arched eyebrow. "Care to explain yourself?"

"Emergency," Emery said. She hopped down and pinched his butt. "Don't worry about it."

"When you rerouted the jet from Vegas a day early, I cut my trip to New York short. It must have been some emergency."

"Oh, it is." Emery glanced at Heidi and giggled.

Heidi rolled her eyes. "Just tell him."

"Heidi's pregnant!"

Jensen barely masked his utter shock. Morgan and I laughed at his face. He was so oblivious sometimes, even when he seemed to see and know everything.

"Congratulations! I assume you're back early to tell Landon."

"Yep. So, don't spoil my surprise."

"I wouldn't dream of it."

Emery leaned her head against his sleeve. "You're the best."

"How did New York go?" Morgan interrupted.

"Colton is great. Thank you for asking," he said with a gleam in his eye.

"Well, yes, I'm sure my nephew is always great, even with *Vanessa*," she said with distaste. "But I meant, with the Van Pelts."

"Did you meet with them?" I asked.

"No, but I met with our lawyers up there since Mor was otherwise occupied. I'm certain they're going to deny Broderick's parole."

"Good." I breathed a sigh of relief.

"I'll be satisfied when I see the paperwork," Morgan said in earnest.

"We'll have it," Jensen assured her.

"I hope this will all be over soon," I said. "In the meantime, I have a baby at home, who I'm missing like crazy."

Morgan smiled. "Get out of here."

I rushed to my car and drove the twenty minutes home, my foot tapping the entire way. It had been forever since I'd been away from Jason this long. Austin had been in rehab the last time I went away without him. And, oh God, I missed Jason! I'd thought I'd be able to suck it up while I was gone. But it had just snuck up on me, and I was kind of glad we were back a day early.

I parked in the garage and raced in the back door. Jenny was sitting on the kitchen floor with Jason banging away at pots and pans.

"Mommy!" Jason cried and dashed toward me.

"Hey, buddy."

He crashed into me, and I enveloped him in my arms, smelling his hair and feeling his little body. A knot formed in my throat, and I swore, I wouldn't cry. But, man, he was so little, and I wanted him to stay like this forever with all the love in his little heart.

I kissed the top of his head and picked him up. "Oh, I missed you!"

He giggled and kissed my cheek.

"How was he?" I asked Jenny.

She got to her feet. "Excellent. As always."

"You were so good for Jen. I guess that means someone deserves a cookie, huh?"

"Cookie!" he cried in excitement.

I got a cookie out for him from the box on the counter and took one for myself. Jenny took one, too, and we both smiled down at my son.

"Thanks for your help. I'll still pay you for the whole weekend," I assured her.

"Anytime, Sut. And you don't have to do that."

"I want to. You had to cancel plans for this. I appreciate it."

She waved me off and hugged Jason one more time before heading out for the day.

Jason and I played all of his favorite games that morning until he finally went down for his nap. I pulled my neglected phone out and dialed David's number.

"How's Vegas, beautiful?"

"I'm home early. When do I get to see you?"

He laughed. "Whenever you're free."

"After this weekend, I bet I can get a sitter whenever I want," I said, thinking about all my friends' enthusiasm about me dating.

"Tomorrow?"

"It's a date."

Twenty-Three

David

It had only been a few short days without Sutton, but it was a few days too many. She was sunshine on a cloudy day. And I was in shadow when she was absent.

I had been eager to leave work to see Sutton. And, if that wasn't enough, Morgan had been acting so strange all day. When I'd tried to ask her about it, she'd clammed up entirely and disappeared. I had no idea what that was about, but I'd figure it out after my date with Sutton.

Julia was at Sutton's and tasked with watching Jason for the night. "Have fun," she said with a wink as I led Sutton out the door.

"Why is everyone acting so weird today?" I asked as I walked her to the car.

Sutton's eyes rounded, and then she shrugged. "Uh...no idea."

I eyed her skeptically but let it go. I was happy she was here. I mean…really, I wanted to skip dinner and take her straight back to my place. After we'd fucked all afternoon last week, I was ready to reenact that. But having her back was good enough. Especially with that smile on her face and that yellow sundress.

Vegas had made her giggly. It was as if she'd suddenly remembered what it had been like before all of her responsibilities. And she seemed lighter. A weight had lifted off her shoulders.

I'd made reservations at West Table for the night, and we got a table next to the window.

"I'm so glad to be home," Sutton said, leaning her elbows on the table and looking up at me with hearts in her eyes.

"Oh, yeah? Was Vegas so bad?"

"No! It was wonderful. But I missed Jason so much. He was so lovey when I came home. I just want to bottle it up and save it for a rainy day."

"I can't imagine him any other way."

"Oh," she said with a snort. "He's in his terrible twos, to be sure. But he's still mine, and I love him. Even when he's a shit."

I laughed. "That makes sense."

"Plus, I liked coming home to you," she said with a grin.

"I can admit that I like you better here than in Las Vegas, probably flirting with a stripper or something."

Sutton choked on the water that she'd been drinking. "I mean…flirting?"

"Oh God, you actually went to a strip club?"

"Shh," she groaned. "I'm not supposed to talk about it."

"Well, now, I want to know everything."

"No way," she said on a giggle. "But I can tell you that Heidi is pregnant."

"She's pregnant? Wow! Is she excited about that?"

"Yes, I guess she and Landon had started trying at the beginning of the summer. She didn't expect it to happen this soon, but here we are. She only found out because she thought she was sick from a hangover, and it was morning sickness."

"Oh shit."

"Yeah. Lots and lots of alcohol." She shrugged, as if to say, *Happens all the time.* "Anyway, we're having a party for them this weekend to celebrate."

"You Wrights use any excuse to have a party, huh?"

"Of course. I mean, technically, you don't even tell most people until you're twelve weeks along, but special circumstances and all. So, we'll party like it's 1999."

"How old were you in 1999?" I asked and laughed when she shrugged.

"Anyway, you should come. It's not a shower or anything, just a party."

"I'd love to be there with you."

She beamed just as the waiter showed up. We ordered our dinner and drinks, and I spent the rest of the meal trying to wrangle more information about Vegas out of her. She never gave an inch, but it was fun to try. She'd had fun. She was in a good mood. That was all that mattered.

I paid the check and then did the thing I'd been wanting to do all night—brought her back to my place.

I'd never had her over to my house before. It was in a country club not that far from her house on the south side of town. I'd come from San Francisco where the house prices were astronomical. With the amount I'd paid for my place here, I could have bought a shoebox there…maybe. I'd gone a little overboard with the promise of a low cost of living.

Sutton's sandals slapped against the hardwood interior as she entered through the front door. "I thought Jensen's house was extravagant for just one person."

"Yeah. It's way too big for only me. But the amenities are worth it."

She smiled. Her eyes latching on to the expensive artwork and carefully curated decorations. "I like it. It suits you. Did you have someone do the interior design?"

"Is it that obvious?"

"Well…most dudes don't have this kind of eye."

"Touché."

I watched her wander around the open floor plan living room and take the whole place in. I wanted to walk over to her, clear off the dining room table, and have my way with her. I was aching for her. I had never felt this feverish about anyone. Ever.

It took every ounce of self-control not to move faster. We'd gone so slow up until last week. I had never been a patient man when it came to anyone or anything other than Sutton. It was a new experience. I relished getting to know her in bits and pieces and putting her together like a puzzle. But I wanted to explore her body. And I didn't want to go slow.

Except I needed to.

I owed it to her to talk first.

I took a deep breath.

"Hey, come sit down with me," I said, gesturing to the couch.

She moseyed back over and sat down. Her legs were jittery, and she eyed my lips once and then twice. She clearly had the same thing on her mind.

"I need to tell you something."

She blushed and looked at her hands. "I kind of need to tell you something, too."

I stalled on the words that were on the tip of my tongue. The words I didn't want to say but needed to get out. "You go first."

"You sure?"

No.

"Yes."

"All right." Sutton took a deep breath. When she glanced back up at me, her cheeks were pink, and she looked embarrassed by whatever she was going to tell me.

"Everything okay?"

"Well, yes." Then, she paused before repeating herself, "Yes. Everything is fine, except that I do have to tell you one thing about Vegas."

"Oh, really?" I asked.

A knot formed in the pit of my stomach. It was Vegas. Who knew what could have happened?

"Yeah. I know I've been tight-lipped about it, but that's because it was Emery's party. It's kind of special, and we wanted to keep it that way." She chewed on her lip. "But I kind of...well...I kind of told everyone that we had sex."

A laugh burst out of my mouth. Of all the things I'd been possibly worried about, that hadn't even crossed my mind.

"You did, what?"

"I know; I know. I mean, it's not like it's a secret, but I kind of shouted it in front of everyone. And then I told everyone what happened—apparently in *vivid* detail."

"How vivid?" I asked, trying to stay serious but a smile remaining on my mouth nonetheless.

"Very. And…that includes Morgan." She winced. "Like, I think I got *really* in-depth with Morgan."

"Oh. Well, that explains that."

"What?"

"Morgan was being super weird today. She was avoiding me, and when I tried to talk to her, she basically ran in the other direction."

"Yeah," Sutton said with a shrug. "I went in-depth with the length and breadth of your dick. She's probably trying not to visualize."

I snorted. "Oh, that's too good. No wonder she's freaking out."

"To be fair, I was really wasted and don't remember the conversation at all."

"It's fine. I think the more important thing is…that you wanted to describe it," I said, leaning forward and pressing a kiss to her lips. "Do you want to start over and pretend to be drunk? I'd be happy to listen to you describe exactly what I did to you in vivid detail."

She scooted across the couch and hiked her leg up and over mine until she was straddling me. "You're not mad?"

"Mad? Definitely no."

"Well…good. I was worried."

"You never have to worry about that. Talk to your girlfriends about your sex life. As long as it's with me, it doesn't bother me."

"Oh, good. Then, maybe I can tell you what I'd like to do to you right now."

I arched an eyebrow. "I'm all ears."

She slid down my lap until she was on her knees between my legs. Her delicate hands moved to my waist and carefully unbuttoned my slacks and dragged the zipper down to the base.

"First, I think I'll have that taste I wanted last week," she said like a little vixen.

I was loving this side of her.

"And second?"

She reached into my boxers and wrapped her hand around my dick. My eyes closed, and I tilted my head back to stifle a groan.

"Oh...you'll find out."

I slipped my pants off and dropped them onto the floor. She licked her lips at the sight of me, and my dick lengthened further in her hand. Fuck. This woman. I was a goner. A total goner.

That first day I'd seen her, I had known she was the one. Even before I knew a single thing about her. She'd looked at me, and I'd been lost. When I'd found out she was a Wright, I had known it would be impossible. Then, married and with a kid. She was completely unreachable. Even worse when Maverick had collapsed. I had gone from a moment in the sun to knowing full well that Sutton Wright would never be mine.

Now, here we were. And it all felt too good to be true.

But I wasn't going to tempt fate.

She wrapped her lips around the head of my cock, and fuck, the entire world was right. Her tongue licked up the shaft until I was slick. It took her a second to work up a rhythm, but once she got into it, it was just like riding a bike apparently. She bobbed up and down, taking me down all the way to the base and then sucking slowly back up. She swirled the head around in her mouth and stroked me up and down. With a tentative grip, she reached for my balls and massaged them in her hand.

My back bucked off the couch. She felt so fucking amazing. I was half-tempted to thrust up into her mouth and take back control. I was teetering on the edge and wanted to take her right there. But she was so fucking enthusiastic on my dick. I wasn't about to change a damn thing she was doing to bring me pleasure. Not when she seemed so happy about it. Not when I was so close to coming and wanted nothing more than to bury my dick inside her to finish.

But, no, she wanted to finish me.

I tapped her head and groaned. "Close."

I didn't want her to think she had to finish, but oh no, that only egged her on. She moved up and down on me until I couldn't hold back anymore. I shot straight up into her mouth, and my vision blurred as my orgasm erupted out of me.

Sutton sat back on her heels and swallowed. It was a beautiful sight.

"Damn, I've been wanting to do that," she said.

"Anytime. Any. Time."

She laughed at my response. I stripped out of my shirt. She tossed her sundress to the side as I directed her into the master bedroom. I had a giant California king bed in the middle of the room. She crawled naked across the cream-patterned duvet with her pert ass in the air.

I grabbed that perfect ass in my hands and yanked her back to the end of the bed. She giggled as she skidded backward. I gingerly flipped her over onto her back, and those beautiful blue eyes looked back up at me with desire.

"Second...I want you inside me," she said breathily. "Right now."

I rolled a condom on and crawled onto the bed before her. She spread her legs and then wrapped them around my waist, tugging me closer. I leaned forward on my elbows and captured her lips. She moaned into my mouth as I pressed the head of my cock against her opening.

"Oh fuck," she said.

"You're so wet."

"Blow jobs get me hot."

"You might be perfect."

She laughed and kissed me again. I thrust into her body until I was fully sheathed inside her. She was wet and warm and tight. God, so tight. She locked her legs behind my body, and then we picked up a rhythm that felt as natural as breathing. In and out, back and forth. *Slap, slap, slap.* It was easy and effortless, and I couldn't believe how fucking incredible she felt. Nothing in this world could ever feel like Sutton right now.

Her breathing turned into pants, and then suddenly, her body locked up, squeezing me as tight as possible. She cried out as she came and sent me straight over the edge. I collapsed forward over her, every drop of me spent.

"Don't ever go away again," I said, kissing her shoulder.

"Never," she agreed. She tilted her head back and sighed softly. "So…uh…what were you going to tell me?"

I placed another kiss on her throat. "Nothing. It doesn't matter."

"You sure?"

"Yeah. This is all that matters."

Twenty-Four

Sutton

Jason animatedly kicked his feet in the car seat. He'd been talking to himself the entire way to Wright Construction. Morgan had reserved the entire top-floor restaurant for Landon and Heidi's pregnancy announcement party. Announcement being an understatement since...everyone already knew about it. But whatever.

I parked out front and hurried around to get him out of the back. He was still mumbling nonstop about something or other. Most times, I could figure out what he was saying and carry on a full conversation with him about it, and sometimes, he was speaking complete gibberish. Today was one of those days.

"Are you ready to see your uncle Landon?" I asked as he helped me unstrap the car seat.

"Yep," he said enthusiastically.

I grinned and helped him out of the car seat. He hopped down and started to rush toward the front door.

I shook my head, caught up to him, and grabbed his hand. "Wait for me."

He gave me this wicked smile that looked just like his daddy. I sighed and then pushed the pain away. I wasn't forgetting Maverick. I never would. I saw him every day in his son. And that was good.

I brushed back Jason's unruly, dark curls. "Let's go together, okay?"

"Okay, Mommy."

I hauled him back to the car, grabbed his bag, and then headed inside. We took the elevator to the top floor, and it opened up to the restaurant. All of the tables had been moved to the perimeter. A buffet had been set up along one wall, and a bar was on the other. Large floor-to-ceiling windows showcased the Lubbock landscape for miles. The building overlooked the Texas Tech campus, and downtown was visible in the other direction. Someone had draped a Congratulations banner over the bar.

Family and friends were gathered together in the space. Everyone looked so happy about the news. And I couldn't deny that I felt the same way. There was something truly special about the possibility of new life. It, like the promise of new love, erased the malaise that followed death. A renewal. One I desperately needed.

"Bethany!" Jason cried.

Of course.

"Let's go see her and Lilyanne," I said.

I wandered across the room to where Bethany, Lilyanne, and Jensen's son, Colton, were seated at a kids table. Colton seemed to be holding court over the others, and I was sure Jason was about to be pulled into his vortex.

"Have fun." I kissed the top of his head.

Annie materialized at my side with a glass of wine.

"You're a goddess," I told her.

"Obviously." She flicked her long red hair over her shoulder. "How awesome is this for Heidi and Landon? Are they finally going to tie the knot?"

"I don't think so. Heidi seemed totally okay with having a kid before getting married. They've been engaged forever. I can't see them rushing it now. If they're happy, what does it matter?"

"It doesn't. I was just curious. Where's your man anyway?"

"He's not here yet," I said with a bubble of excitement and anticipation sweeping through me.

Both of us had been swamped all week with work. Plus, Jenny had finally decided to take the plunge to get into pharmacy school and was studying to take the PCAT, so she couldn't take any extra night shifts. And I didn't blame her one bit. She wanted to be a pharmacist, and the work was a lot. Just like Annie starting medical school next week. My two best friends were amazing. I dreaded the day that Jenny would leave me and Jason, but it had to happen eventually.

Either way, it meant that I hadn't seen David since our last date, and I missed him. This would be our first event together as a couple. Officially.

"Okay, good," Annie said conspiratorially.

I dragged my attention back to her. "Oh God, why?"

"Well, while I have you to myself, I want you to tell me everything you know about Jensen's friend."

My eyes swept the room until they landed on my oldest brother. He was talking to Emery, but standing next to them was a man I had never seen before in my life. But I knew immediately why he'd drawn Annie's attention.

He was hot. Like on-fire hot. Greek god hot. Chiseled-out-of-marble, too-gorgeous-to-be-real, jaw-dropping hot.

My cheeks flamed as I looked at him. There was something about him that exuded confidence. The cut of his tailored black suit. The crisp blue tie knotted at this throat. The sweep of his cerulean eyes as he took the room in. An awareness of himself that was in every twitch of his jaw, quirk of his mouth, and movement of his hands.

He had a presence. I knew that people said that about my brothers, but I guessed I was immune to them. I was not immune to this guy. He had something. That *it* factor that could not be bought or learned. It was inherent. It was born and bred into the person.

"I don't know who that is," I finally said.

"Damn! I was hoping you'd offer me an introduction."

"Didn't you just sleep with my cousin?"

Annie shrugged. "That was, like…weeks ago, Sut. Plus, he's back in Vancouver. What fun am I going to have with that?"

"You're incorrigible."

"Duh. That's why you love me." She batted her lashes at me. "Now…introduction?"

"I cannot believe you're dragging me into this. You don't need my help to meet him."

"No, but I'm not close enough to see if he has a ring on. And a guy that attractive has to be married, right?"

"I've no idea. But, honestly, when has that ever stopped you before?"

Annie thought about it. "Fair point."

I laughed and rolled my eyes at her, but I was a good friend. I walked her over to Jensen and Emery to meet this mysterious man. He was even taller in person, and his hair shone from the afternoon sun. He was the kind of guy who could easily make you tongue-tied.

"Sutton," Jensen said with a smile. "I'm glad you're here. I wanted you to meet a friend from when I lived in New York City. This is Penn."

Penn extended his hand toward me, and I swapped out my wine glass to shake his. I noticed that his other hand had no ring on it.

"Penn Kensington, pleasure to meet you," he said with a dazzling smile.

"Hi," I said. Annie nudged me. "This is my friend Annie."

He took her hand, too, and she simpered and smiled. But he was polite and ever the gentleman. At least he was acting like it...and he looked like it...but somehow, I knew he wasn't. He most certainly was not a gentleman.

"How did you two meet?" I asked.

"We ran in the same circles," Jensen said, not elaborating. That likely meant his ex-wife, Vanessa, had modeling connections to Penn or at least to the

Kensingtons. "But we've kept in touch over the years. His mother is the mayor of New York City."

"Wow!" I said. "That's pretty incredible."

Penn shrugged. "She enjoys it."

No love lost there apparently.

"Penn was here for a philosophy symposium and gave a lecture at Tech today. He looked me up when he was in town. It was good timing."

"I was trying to convince him to come back for the wedding," Emery said.

"With your girlfriend?" Annie asked shamelessly.

"I hope I can make it." Then, Penn smiled. "Though I don't have a girlfriend."

"You're more than welcome," Emery added. "Jensen invited the entire fucking town, so…we have space."

I snorted and then covered my mouth. Emery had made her distaste for the size of the wedding abundantly clear. It was going to be a behemoth of a thing, but everyone knew Jensen Wright. Hotels were sold out for the occasion. It was bigger than a Texas Tech football game. It was a good thing it was happening before the season started.

"That's kind of you," Penn said. "I'd love to be there."

My eyes snagged over Penn's shoulder, and I watched David walk in the room. My heart fluttered. He looked handsome in khakis and a button-up. His eyes were searching me out. I waved to draw his attention, and his return smile was gorgeous. It had been a long week without him. He rushed across the room toward me.

"Excuse me," I said and then weaved around Penn and met David.

192

He pulled me into a hug. "I missed you."

"I know," I agreed. "Maybe we could go somewhere alone."

He laughed. "That eager, huh?"

"Aren't you?"

"I am," he confirmed.

"What took you so long? I thought you left before me?"

"Katherine called. She keeps trying to get me to come see her, and I'm not ready for that."

"I think you owe it to her to try. Just because she sides with your parents doesn't mean you should shut her out forever."

He shrugged. "Yeah. Maybe."

"You don't want to be estranged from your sibling. I don't know how I'd survive without mine."

"True. Your situation is really different," he said with a wince. "Don't worry about it."

"I want you to be happy."

Something shifted in his appearance. Like he wanted to say something more, but he held back.

"Everything else okay?" I asked.

He nodded. "Yeah. Can we talk after this?"

"You can't ask a girl that and leave her hanging."

"It's not bad," he assured me with a laugh. "I want some more time with you."

"Well, I have Jason."

"It'll be quick."

"Okay," I agreed.

Though nerves hit me in the pit of my stomach. He seemed…off. I'd never had this feeling from him before. He was always so calm and soothing. And, now, he seemed jittery. I didn't know what to expect and hoped it really was nothing.

"In the meantime," I said, grabbing his arm and pulling him back toward Jensen, "come meet Jensen's hot friend, who Annie is going to try to sleep with tonight."

David laughed, all the stress leaving his shoulders again. "Who doesn't Annie try to sleep with?"

"You, I hope."

"No worries there."

We walked back into the circle, and I opened my mouth to introduce David as the CFO of Wright Construction. But Penn was grinning from ear to ear, and he wasn't looking at me. He was staring at David. And David was staring back in abject horror.

"What are the fucking chances of seeing you here?" Penn asked in shock. "I was just talking to your sister yesterday about how I haven't seen you in so fucking long. And, now, here you are."

"Uh...Penn," David said. His eyes shifted from side to side, as if he was trying to find a way to escape this meeting.

"You know each other?" I asked in confusion.

I looked back and forth between them. *How did Penn know Katherine and David? From San Francisco?*

"Are you kidding?" Penn asked with a laugh. "We grew up together in New York. No one quite like David Van Pelt."

Twenty-Five

David

D avid. Van. Pelt.
	Those words.
Those fucking words.

I'd avoided them for so long. Put my past behind me. Hidden it, concealed it, literally court order–sealed my name away so that it would disappear into thin air. Float away like ashes from a burning building.

But I couldn't run forever. Not from this apparently. No matter how far I ran, that name always caught up with me. And, now, it was here. In Lubbock, Texas. Ruining everything again.

It wasn't enough that my father was in prison for God only knew how long. Or that my mother had been implicated in the family bullshit but managed to stay out of jail. Or that Katherine sided with them and not me. None of it mattered. Only my last name.

Seven fucking letters that crashed a bulldozer through the Wright party.

Silence followed Penn's proclamation.

Wide-eyed stares.

Jaws dropped open.

Tension roiled through the crowd.

Penn quickly realized he'd made a mistake. He was an expert at judging a crowd. He'd ruled them for a time in New York. I could see he was trying to find a way to backpedal. But there was no way out of this.

I'd made my bed. Now, I had to lie in it.

"Sutton," I said, taking a step toward her.

She flinched as if I'd struck her.

Her eyes were disbelieving. A window to her confusion and denial. She seemed to be trying to reconcile this news. To make it fit together. But it didn't fit. It would never fit.

I'd been planning to tell her. I'd tried to so many times. It had never been the right moment…and now, it never would be.

"What is he talking about?" Sutton managed to get out.

"Yeah…why did he call you Van Pelt?" Jensen asked.

I could barely look at him. Jensen, who had trusted me and believed in me, who had gotten me this job. Who I knew would never forgive me for the words that were about to come out of my mouth.

"Because that's my name," I told him. "Or…it was."

"But…how?" Jensen demanded. "We ran a background check. We were thorough."

"Court-sealed name change. It doesn't show up anywhere. Not even background checks."

Jensen looked flabbergasted. As if no one had ever deceived him like this. Not in matters of business.

"Hey, I'm sorry," Penn said. "I didn't know that you'd had your name changed. Katherine didn't mention anything."

"Would she have really said something?" I asked, knowing my sister and her plans to make her still look like the Upper East Side princess that she'd grown up as.

"I figured at least to me."

"It's fine," I said. Not Penn's fault. It was mine.

I saw everything burning down around me. Jensen knew. Sutton knew. Morgan would soon know. *Would I have a job? A girlfriend? A life here in Lubbock? Would anyone forgive me for trying to be someone else?*

Their faces said no. And I didn't know why I'd expected anything else. They'd been saying all summer how much they detested the Van Pelts. I'd snuck into their midst, undetected, and now, I would have to reap the consequences of that duplicity. Whatever they might be...

"It's not fine," Sutton said.

Her expression was raw. Pain written across her entire body. Pain I'd caused.

"No, I meant—"

"I don't care what you meant," she said harshly. She waved her hand in front of her. "You're a *Van Pelt*. You've known all along. You *played* us. You...you played *me*."

"Sutton, I didn't—"

"You did!" she cried.

Eyes were drawn to us, and I could tell the party was slowly realizing that a fight was happening. Right here in the middle of Landon and Heidi's pregnancy party.

I didn't want to lose everything. Not again. Not after I'd gone through it twice already. I couldn't walk away from this job like I had the one in San Francisco. I couldn't walk away from this family like I'd done in New York. And I sure as hell couldn't walk away from Sutton. I'd never met anyone else like her.

"Please let me try to explain," I pleaded.

"Explain?" She clutched her chest as if I were causing her physical pain. "There's no explanation. There are no excuses. You deceived us on purpose. You knew what had happened with the Van Pelts. Even if you didn't know, you found out on the Fourth of July. Oh God…is that what Katherine's call was about? The parole?"

I nodded mutely.

"Christ. I'm such an idiot. We're all idiots. You've been here over a year. You could have told someone. You could have told me."

"I wanted to. I tried."

"Oh, I'm sure."

I swallowed back my frustration. She had every right to yell at me. I'd never lied to her, but I hadn't ever been forthright about my past.

And, now, the party was closing in. I could see Austin, Landon, and Morgan drifting our way. I knew, as soon as they were in proximity, with all the Wrights in one place…I was done. I was out of here. I just needed to…to do something. To make her understand.

"Can we talk about this?"

She shook her head and glanced away from me.

"Sutton," Jensen said softly, "maybe we should move this to the conference room."

"No," she said, staring down her brother. She was a fire-breathing dragon, and not even Jensen could withstand the look of pain on her face. "No, we're having this out now."

"What's going on?" Morgan asked. She had skipped over the quickest and was giving Jensen a questioning look.

"We have a...new development that we should take downstairs."

"David is a Van Pelt," Sutton said, throwing her hand out at me. "I mean...is anything you told me true?"

"Wait...what?" Morgan asked.

"Yes. Everything I said was true," I assured her. "Just...not the whole truth."

"You tried to build a relationship on lies. White lies are still lies. You omitted who you are, and you did it on purpose."

Her words were a viper strike cutting across my skin.

They hurt the worst because they were true.

"What's all the fuss about over here?" Austin said, finally joining the circle with Landon.

"Yeah. What's with the yelling?" Landon asked.

"We're trying to figure that out," Morgan said.

"Oh no. There's a perfectly reasonable explanation for all of this," Sutton said. "David lied to us for a year. He's a con artist. He pretended to be someone he's not."

Austin looked back and forth between Sutton and me, as if he wasn't sure who he should be sticking up for.

"David is a Van Pelt," Sutton said point blank.

The circle silenced again at her announcement. It was awful to watch the hurt in Morgan's eyes. The loathing in Austin's. The confusion in Landon's. And, worst of all, Sutton's…so hurt that she was lashing out. I wanted to make it better, but I was the one who had hurt her.

"I'm really sorry to have brought this up," Penn said again. "David is a great guy. I can vouch for him and Katherine. They're not like their parents."

"You really are a Van Pelt," Jensen said with a shake of his head.

"I was," I corrected.

"How could you do this to me?" Sutton asked.

A tear slipped down her cheek, and I watched my butterfly's wings get clipped. She'd put herself out there after everything that happened, and I'd ruined it. I'd thought I could heal her, but I'd only made it worse.

"You bastard," Austin said.

He launched himself toward me. I took a stuttering step backward, but he reared back and punched me in the face.

"Fuck," I cried. I covered my face and took another step away from him.

"Austin!" Morgan yelled.

"Stop it!" I heard from Landon.

But Austin was still coming. It took both of his brothers to restrain him. He was spitting mad.

"I told you I would kill you if you hurt her. You clearly didn't listen."

I had no words. I'd said I wouldn't, and I had.

Sutton scampered forward and put herself between me and Austin before I could ever get words out. "Stop it. Just leave him alone."

Hope glimmered in my conscience. Maybe...maybe there was still a chance. I could explain why I'd had those papers sealed, why I'd changed my name to begin with. I could tell her all the things I'd been holding back. Make her understand.

But her eyes were empty when they looked at me. "Sutton—"

"You should go," she said.

"Please, let me explain. My parents—"

She held up her hand. "No. Just...just go."

"What about us?" I managed to get out. I could hardly breathe, waiting there for the answer I knew was coming.

"What us?"

A ten-ton weight dropped on my chest.

A tear slipped down her cheek, and she brushed it away.

The distance between us ballooned.

"I don't know who you are, David," she whispered, her voice finally cracking. The pain finally edging into her speech. "There is no us."

Thud.

The sound of her heart closing back up.

Crack.

The sound of the world opening up and swallowing me.

Snap.

201

The sound of my new reality. Alone.

The End

Acknowledgments

Thank you to everyone who put their hands on this manuscript. I needed a lot of help, especially with Jason in this. I don't have kids, and I had to rely on my eighteen-month-old niece a lot in hopes that she was like an average two-year-old. (I don't think that she is. LOL.) Thanks to Facebook people for advice on children in general. And I'm so sorry to all of the people I know recently who have lost a dear loved one. I've thankfully not had a lot of loss in my life, and reading other's grief really influenced this story. I wanted Sutton's pain to be authentic, and I had to dig deep for that. My little butterfly needed to fly.

I can't wait for all of you to read the conclusion to Sutton and David's story in *The Wright One* and see how all this madness plays out! As always, thank you for going on this ride with me!

About the Author

K.A. Linde is the *USA Today* bestselling author of the Avoiding Series and more than twenty other novels. She grew up as a military brat and attended the University of Georgia where she obtained a Master's in political science. She works full-time as an author and loves dancing, binge-watching *Supernatural*, and traveling in her spare time.

She currently lives in Lubbock, Texas, with her husband and two super-adorable puppies.

Visit her online at www.kalinde.com and on Facebook, Twitter, and Instagram @authorkalinde.

Join her newsletter at www.kalinde.com/subscribe for exclusive content, free books, and giveaways every month.

The conclusion to the sexy contemporary romance duet from *USA Today* bestselling author K.A. Linde...

The
Wright
One

(WRIGHT LOVE DUET, #2)

Secrets swarm all around. My world is crumbling under the strain. I don't know if we can survive this.

My heart is in the Wright place. But is his?

The Wright One is the last book in the Wright Love Duet. Find out if Sutton and David survive their world of secrets in the conclusion to the Wright Love duet!

COMING MAY 29TH!

Made in the USA
Columbia, SC
01 June 2018